Pizza with Extra Creeps

Look for these SpineChillers™

Dr. Shivers' Carnival of Terror
Attack of the Killer House
The Venom Versus Me

SPINE CHILLERS™

Pizza with Extra Creeps

Fred E. Katz

Publishers Since 1798

THOMAS NELSON PUBLISHERS
Nashville • Atlanta • London • Vancouver

Published in Nashville, Tennessee, by Thomas Nelson, Inc., Publishers, and distributed in Canada by Word Communications, Ltd., Richmond, British Columbia. SpineChillers™ is a trademark of Thomas Nelson, Inc., Publishers.

Editor: Lila Empson; Copyeditor: Nedra Lambert; Packaging: Kevin Farris, Belinda Bass; Production: Brenda White, Lori Gliko.

ISBN 0-7852-7486-3

Printed in the United States of America.

1 2 3 4 5 6 — 01 00 99 98 97 96

1

It was another new house and another new town. I was getting used to having a new bedroom and attending a new school and a new church every year or two.

Dad worked for a big company with offices nationwide. He did well there. His boss valued him. He transferred Dad to wherever the company was having trouble. This time it was Riverdale.

I liked the new house. My room here was bigger than my rooms in any of the other houses we had lived in. The room next to mine was my brother Tommy's nursery. Dad and Mom's room was down a long hallway from my room.

Dad had already put my sign on my bedroom door. It told everyone this was MAX'S ROOM. I was named after my dad. He is Maxwell Walker and so am I. Mom calls him Maxie. She didn't like the name "Junior" or "Little Maxie," though. She decided to call me Max. Dad calls me Buddy. I like that. It makes me feel very close to him.

It was Saturday and I was busy unpacking boxes. I

removed my baseball card collection from one of the boxes and placed it on the bookshelf in my bedroom. I had some great cards. Dad had been collecting for years, and he gave me his collection. I was the only kid I knew with a Mickey Mantle and a Hank Aaron. Dad was great about helping me find the best cards.

When I finished the cards, I grabbed the box with my books in it. My favorite set was The Chronicles of Narnia by C. S. Lewis. Mom read them to me when I was young, but I went through them again. They were really interesting. As I stacked my books on the bed, our dog, Snowball, padded into the room.

Snowball was a white puff of fur. When we had talked about getting a dog I had wanted a big dog. But Mom said because we moved so much and might not always have a fenced backyard, we should get a small dog that we could keep in the house. So we got Snowball, a bichon frise. He's small, and he's my best friend.

Just like Dad called me Buddy, I called Snowball Buddy. It made him sound tougher. One look at him and people knew that he wasn't tough at all.

Snowball jumped on the bed and knocked over the stack of books. They went all over the floor.

"Buddy, get off the bed. I'm working here," I scolded.

He just looked at me and tilted his head from side to side, listening to me. I sometimes thought he understood what I said to him. This time, though, he didn't care if I needed to put away my books. He wanted to play. To be honest, that was what I wanted to do as well.

I placed my forearms on the bed. I once saw a TV show that said this position was the international dog sign that meant "play." He imitated me then jumped off the bed and ran down the stairs. I was in hot pursuit.

I followed Snowball into the family room where Mom and Dad were busy unpacking boxes.

Dad glanced up at me. "How's your unpacking coming, Buddy?"

"It was going pretty good. That is, until Snowball decided to 'help' me. He scattered my books all over the place."

Mom laughed. She called Snowball over to her and rubbed him behind his ears. "Poor Snowball. None of us have paid much attention to him today, what with all this unpacking."

Snowball wagged his tail as Mom scratched him under his chin.

"Max, will you please take that box to the attic for me?" Mom pointed to some boxes in the corner of the room. "The one marked Christmas decorations. I don't think we have room for it in any of the closets."

"Sure thing, Mom." I picked up the box. "Come on, Buddy. You can go with me."

Snowball scampered behind me as I carried the box to the attic steps.

The stairs to the attic were dark and creaky. Each

one I climbed sounded like it was saying back to me, "Get off. I'm old. I hurt when you walk on me."

Of course, that was just my imagination. My parents thought I had an overactive imagination. When I was a little kid I thought there were monsters in my bedroom. Before going to sleep at night I always asked Mom and Dad to look under my bed and in my closet. They always assured me there were no monsters hiding in my room.

I had the feeling that my new house would have plenty of things in it that would engage my imagination. After all, it was a big house with lots of rooms to explore.

As I climbed the attic stairs, I heard a noise. I stopped and listened. *That was not my imagination.*

I moved up another stair and held by breath to listen. I heard it again. A rush of fear prickled my skin. Something was in the attic.

I thought of going down to get Dad, but then he might think it was me imagining things again. Dad thought it was something that I ate that caused my imagination to go into overdrive. He would always say, "You better cut down on the pizza with extra creeps."

I had to explore this one myself. Besides, I had my trusty and faithful protector and sidekick with me.

Or so I thought.

I looked around for Snowball. He wasn't behind me. Apparently he had found something more interesting to do.

I thought about calling him, but I did not want to make any noise that might scare away the intruder before I could catch him, her, or it. I was not sure why I thought I should or could catch whatever was in our attic.

I took another step and listened. The intruder must have heard me. A crashing sound sent chills up my spine. The thing in our attic must have moved quickly and broken something. I wasn't sure I should go any farther, but I wasn't going to be a fraidy cat either.

I took another step. I was high enough to see into the attic. I had hoped that the sunlight would be shining into the attic. From where I stood I could see that the windows were so dirty that very little sunlight could filter through.

I glanced around the dimly lit attic, but I did not see any sign of the intruder. What really had me worried was how I was going to get into the attic without the intruder seeing me. I had to be prepared.

I saw an old piece of wood lying on the attic floor. If I could get to the wood then I would have something I could use to defend myself.

The noise distracted me again. It was like a great whistling or the sound of wind in a horrible thunderstorm. I had to make my move. I tried to remember everything I had ever seen in those karate movies.

I jumped up to the top stair. I set the box on the floor then dived toward the piece of wood. My body slammed against the exposed wood in the slanted attic wall. It hurt, but I was able to grab my protection device.

I could make out a few shapes in the darkness. They appeared to be old trunks. The former owners must have left them here when they moved. I imagined they were filled with great stuff to play with. Maybe some old pirate put a treasure map in one of them. I made a mental note to come back up here with a flashlight.

I slowly crawled toward one of the shapes. It was a large storage trunk. I hid behind it.

I took a deep breath and looked around the side of the trunk.

Someone was standing about three feet from me.

I didn't think that the intruder saw me. He did not move toward me. I had to attack him before he attacked me.

I rolled from behind the trunk and leaped to my feet. I raised the wooden board to clobber the intruder.

That's when I got a good look. The person I saw in the dark was not a person at all. It was a sewing dummy that people used to piece together clothing they were sewing.

"Sorry, sir," I said aloud. "I hope that I did not scare you." I laughed at my joke.

I pushed my way past the dummy. Out of the corner of my eye I saw something move. I froze and held my breath. I slipped behind the sewing model.

The whistling noise began again, and again I saw something move. I could only make out the corner of it. It looked like yellowish-white material. I could see through it.

As far as I knew, there was only one thing that was

whitish and transparent. The Walker house had a ghost living in the attic.

I got down on all fours and crawled on the dusty floor toward the ghost. I wanted to see it, but I was not very excited about it confronting me. I was not sure what ghosts did to people. I had seen them in movies. I had read about them in horror stories. But I didn't know what real ghosts did to people in real life.

I crawled a few steps closer. Then I heard a sound behind me. *How in the world did I get myself into this mess?* I thought. I had a ghost only a few feet in front of me, and now some other kind of creature was creeping up behind me.

I sucked in a deep breath and let it out slowly. I was in trouble. I remembered reading that the best defense is a good offense. I had my piece of wood, and that gave me a strong offense. I had to attack.

I jumped up and leaped toward the ghost. As I catapulted forward, I realized what a stupid move it was. Ghosts are supposed to be able to move through walls. What would a scrap of wood wielded by a middle schooler do but pass right through it?

It was too late. I had the ghost in my sights. I raced forward holding the board in an attack position.

I skidded to a quick stop on the dusty floor. I looked at the ghost. Then I could not control myself any longer. I broke out in giggles. My ghost was an old, tattered curtain that was being moved by the wind blowing through a broken windowpane.

I walked closer and saw jagged, broken pieces of glass on the floor beneath the window. I wondered what could have broken the attic window. I peered out and saw that the large tree in our front yard stretched its limbs up to the height of the house. One of the branches must have crashed through the window during a storm.

That mystery was solved and I started to relax when the sound I heard behind me started again. It was a very high-pitched growl.

I picked up my wooden protector and started back in the direction of the steps. There wasn't any light coming through on that side of the attic so I knew that the growling was not the wind blowing through another broken window. This had to be a living creature.

I went into a crouch so that the creature could not attack me easily in the dark. With each step my heart beat faster. What was I about to face?

I came near the steps. The creature was lurking near them. It was now the moment of truth.

I dropped onto my hands and knees again and approached the beast. I stuck my head around the trunk.

The creature leaped for me.

I put out my arms and caught the flying monster. As soon as it hit my chest I closed my arms around it. Then I felt the wet, sloppy lick of Snowball's tongue on my face.

"Thanks, Buddy, for the scare of my life. I've got to put a bell on your collar. That way you can't sneak up on me."

I gave the white ball of fur a hug and set him down on the attic floor. "Come on, boy. Not much to see up here. Although we do need to come back one day and look through these trunks. Remember, if we find a map to buried treasure, we split it fifty-fifty. That ought to keep you in treats and dog food for a long time."

As I walked down the stairs, I started thinking that maybe my parents were right. I did have a hyperactive imagination, especially after consuming massive amounts of pizza with extra cheese.

Now that I had checked out the attic it was time to head to the underground cavern called the basement.

Earlier, I had helped Dad carry some boxes to the basement. We looked around a little, but I had not thoroughly explored the area.

Mom wanted to turn the basement into a playroom. As I looked around at the basement walls I saw she had her work cut out for her.

The walls were plain cement blocks. They were coated with a very thin layer of paint. Dad had said they were whitewashed. I had heard the term before, but I didn't know what it meant. He explained that whitewash is a mixture of paint and water.

None of the lights in the basement had wall switches. The individual bulbs had to be turned on and off with pull chains that hung down from the ceiling.

One little room in the basement still had a dirt floor. Dad explained that many, many years ago this room had been the coal cellar. The house once had a coal furnace and this was where the coal was kept. The wall where the coal chute door used to be was now bricked in with cement blocks.

I had thought the idea of a coal furnace was pretty cool. Then Dad told me that when my grandfather was my age he lived in a house that had a coal furnace. He had to get up in the middle of the night in the cold winter to shovel coal into the furnace. After hearing that story I was glad our house now had a gas furnace.

The furnace was big and ugly. When Dad had turned it on to test it, it had made a loud belching noise. We both had laughed and said, "Excuse me," when it did that.

The ductwork that carried the warm air in the winter was tucked up in the ceiling of the basement. The ducts spread everywhere along the rafters. This made the furnace look like a big robot with long arms that hugged the house.

Now that I was in the basement without my dad, I thought the coal cellar looked really spooky. The one small lightbulb that hung from the center of the ceiling did little to illuminate the room. Instead it seemed to only cast eerie shadows against the walls.

As I was looking around, I felt something brush by me. I thought I saw something move, but I wasn't sure because it was too dark. Snowball must have noticed it, too. He ran out the cellar door and started barking at something behind the furnace.

For a second I felt scared. Then I told myself, "Hey, you're twelve years old. That's too old to be scared of a basement. You probably just saw a mouse."

Since I had made such a fool of myself in the attic by making up frightening beings in my imagination I moved ahead, feeling a little braver. I went over to where Snowball was barking and looked behind the furnace. But it was too dark back there to see anything.

I tried to reassure myself that my furry best friend was yelping at nothing more than a mouse. I decided that I should tell Dad about the mouse.

"Hey, Dad," I called out as I climbed the steps.

"Yeah, Buddy?" he answered.

"I think Snowball found a mouse in the basement." I felt pretty brave by then.

"Let's go check it out," he said to me. We descended the stairs together.

He called to Mom, "Kathy, where's the broom?" He was looking behind the boxes for it. "Forget it. I found it." He turned to me and said, "Let's go on a hunting expedition. You can be the world famous big game hunter and I'll be your gun bearer."

That was one of the things I really loved about Dad. He always made everything fun.

Snowball had stopped barking and was now sniffing around the bottom edge of the furnace. Dad and I looked all around the furnace, but we didn't see anything.

"The mouse must be hiding behind the furnace," I said.

"Let's look back there and see," Dad responded.

We crawled as far back behind the furnace as we could. Since I was smaller than Dad I was able to crawl in a little farther than he could.

All of a sudden, Snowball started to bark again.

Dad and I scrambled out from behind the furnace. With the broom in my hand I walked to where Snowball was barking at the door to the coal cellar.

Dad said, "Maybe the mouse is in there." He was heading for the door when I stopped him.

"Dad, when I was down here before I went in that

room. I don't remember shutting the door. But now it's closed. I'm beginning to think that this thing isn't a mouse." I was starting to feel afraid again.

Dad walked to the door and paused. Each step he took made me more frightened. I held on to the broom so tightly that my hands started to cramp.

Dad reached for the doorknob. I raised the broom like it was a baseball bat. I was ready to clobber any monster that hid behind that door. Dad's hand turned the knob and the door creaked slowly open.

I looked inside from my safe distance. Dad walked in with Snowball standing guard behind him. The dog held his head like he had cornered a wild animal.

Dad reached up for the chain on the light. I didn't remember shutting the light off either. How did that happen? Who could have turned it off? My heart started pumping hard.

Dad pulled the chain, but the light didn't come on. Snowball came running out of the room and passed me. By the time I turned around, Snowball was standing by the furnace again, barking his head off.

Dad walked out of the cellar.

"The lightbulb's dead," he said. "We'll probably have to replace all the bulbs in the basement. Did you see the mouse?"

"No. But Snowball must have seen something," I

answered. Snowball was still barking frantically at the furnace.

"I think we should set out some mousetraps," Dad said. "We can buy some of those 'humane' traps. The kind that catches the mouse alive. Then we can let it go in the woods behind the house."

Dad started walking to the stairs. "Come on, Buddy. Let's have some dinner. We'll worry about the mouse tomorrow."

I called Snowball but he ignored me. He was still busy sniffing around the furnace. I knelt down and picked him up in my arms and carried him up the stairs.

For dinner Mom had ordered a pizza with extra cheese. That was my favorite part of moving. We got to eat pizza for three days straight. That's usually how long it took us to unpack all the boxes.

The last time we moved I hid a few of the kitchen boxes in the garage. I hoped I could get a few more pizzas out of the move. Mom found them though. She wasn't very happy with my joke that time. Besides, sometimes I had very weird dreams after eating so much pizza with extra cheese.

After dinner Dad gave Tommy his bath and put him to bed. By the time he got back downstairs Mom and I had hooked up the TV. We wanted to see the Cubs game. When we lived in Chicago we went to see them play several times. They were Mom and Dad's favorite team. My favorite was the Los Angeles Dodgers.

17

We had never lived there but I followed the team faithfuly.

When the game ended, all three of us were tired and ready to go to bed. I headed up to my room.

I had forgotten the books were still all over the floor. I kicked them aside and put on my pj's.

Snowball and I jumped into bed. He liked my pillow so we fought for it a few minutes and then decided to share it on his terms. He wrapped his body around my head. I would sleep with a white fur hat on my head that night.

As I lay in bed I thought about what might be in the basement. I hadn't seen whatever it was, but Snowball had sure seen something. The thumping in my chest told me our spooky visitor was no mouse.

6

Morning came. Dad made breakfast while Mom got Tommy ready for church.

I picked out one of my coolest T-shirts. The one with a skateboard on it. About three pancakes through breakfast, Mom looked over and noticed the shirt. That was when she gave me one of her get-serious looks.

"Max, I think the first day at a new church requires a better shirt than that. And before you say, 'Ah, Mom,' just go change it," she said. I knew there wasn't much chance of me arguing my point.

After breakfast I changed my shirt and we all got in the car to head to the church.

The new church was bigger than any we had gone to before. My Sunday school class had about twenty-five other junior high students in it. Everyone was really friendly.

The teacher's name was Keith Bonhat. He greeted me warmly and introduced me to the class. He told me he liked to play basketball. I thought that was appropriate because he was a tall man. I thought he was cool.

One of the guys in the class was named Jamal. He joked around a lot. He was funny. Jamal was a little smaller than the other students. After class when we talked he told me he had an older brother and sister. They were in the senior high class.

I liked Jamal. He made me feel comfortable. And he introduced me to some of the other middle schoolers in the class.

One guy Jamal introduced me to was Aaron Jordan. He liked basketball almost as much as Keith. Because his last name was Jordan, some kids called him "Air." He liked his nickname since he shared it with Michael Jordan.

Jamal, Aaron, and I went into the fellowship hall to join the other class members for donuts and drinks. As I was pouring myself a glass of orange juice one of the girls from the class walked up to me.

"Hi, I'm Eve." She smiled when she said it.

I get real nervous when I meet people for the first time. My mouth went dry, but I managed to mumble my name. "I'm Max."

"I know. Keith introduced you at the beginning of class," she reminded me.

"Oh, yeah, I forgot," I said.

She was very nice and kept talking to me. "So, where did you move from?"

"We used to live outside Chicago." I was feeling a little more comfortable now.

"Where do you live now?" She seemed interested.

"On Washington Street," I replied.

"Oh, really? I live on Washington Street, too!"

"We bought the big house with the white fence around it," I said.

"The witch house," she said.

"Which house? The big one with the fence around it," I repeated myself.

"The witch house," she said again, nodding as if she had understood what I had just said.

"Which house? You know, the one with the big fence and the weird mailbox out front." I started to think that maybe she wasn't too bright.

"Yeah, the witch house," she said again.

"I already told you three times which house it is." I was getting frustrated.

"Wait a second. You think I'm saying which, w-h-i-c-h. I'm saying witch, w-i-t-c-h. A witch used to live in that house," she stated.

"A what? You've got to be kidding me." What she said scared me a little, but I didn't want to show it. I wanted to know what she meant by "witch house." Just then Jamal walked over and she turned to him.

"Jamal, Max moved into the witch house on Washington Street. You've heard the stories about it, haven't you?" she asked.

"Yeah, lots of spooky stuff used to happen around

that house. I heard some kids disappeared that lived near it. Bones were found in the woods behind the house. It looked like they had been cooked. She must have made stew with them. That's why they ran the old woman out of the house," Jamal said.

It was lousy timing when my parents walked up, ending the conversation. It was time to go to the worship service.

I couldn't concentrate on the service, though. All I could think about was that I lived in the "witch house." I wondered if the old witch would come back and make stew out of me.

For Sunday lunch I got to have my favorite again—pizza with extra cheese.

During the meal I was lost in my thoughts. I remembered what Jamal had said about the missing kids and the bones found in the woods behind our house.

"Buddy, you've hardly said a word." Dad gave me a concerned look. It was unusual for me to be so quiet. "What's on your mind?" He picked up his napkin and began to wipe off the pizza sauce from Tommy's face.

I wanted to ask Mom and Dad if they had heard anything about the witch. But I didn't want them to think I was scared. I decided to play it cool.

"Oh . . . uh . . . I was just thinking about the kids I met at church this morning."

Mom reached for another slice of pizza. "Did you make some new friends?"

"Yes. Everyone in my class was real nice."

"Who were the three kids you were talking to when we came to get you for the church service?" Mom asked.

23

"The smaller guy is Jamal. The other guy is named Aaron. And the girl's name is Eve." I took a sip of iced tea.

"Oh, that reminds me . . . they told me something about our house that really shocked me." I was still trying to play it cool.

"Oh? What's that?" Dad asked.

"Well, Eve called this place the witch house." I tried to maintain a calm expression. "Have either of you heard anything about a witch?"

"A witch?" Mom had a surprised expression. "Where would she get an idea like that? Maxie, have you heard any rumors about a witch?"

Dad swallowed a bite of pizza. "No, I haven't. I did hear that an older woman lived here before. But nothing about her being a witch." He looked at me. "Don't worry about it, son. Every old house has stories about ghosts and goblins."

"Oh, I'm not scared or anything. I was just a little surprised by her story." I paused for a moment. I needed to change the subject to convince them I wasn't scared. "By the way, there's a youth group meeting tomorrow night. Can I go?"

"Absolutely. I'll drive you. Maybe I can meet your new friends," Dad said.

"Great. Well, if you'll excuse me, I think I'll go upstairs and restack all my books. And I've still got some unpacking to do."

Before I went up to my room to finish putting my

books away I looked around for Snowball. I found him on the deck in our backyard, taking his afternoon nap in the sun. Just one of the many he took during the day. I figured I could stack my books now without any interruptions.

I climbed the steps to my room. As I reached the door, I suddenly had an odd feeling. It was the same feeling I had when Dad had opened the coal cellar door. The feeling that someone, or something, was behind the door.

I took a deep breath to calm down. I felt like a real chicken. In my fear, I grabbed the doorknob and flung it open.

I saw a black figure go flying through the air. I jumped back and slammed the door shut. For a few moments I stood there like I was frozen. I felt as if my feet were glued to the floor. My mouth was dry. It took me a few seconds to get moisture back in my mouth. I swallowed. Then I screamed.

Dad came rushing up the stairs. "What is it, Buddy?" he yelled to me.

"Dad, there was something in my room. I saw it. It was black and it flew by the doorway really fast. I don't know what it was, but I saw something." I was talking too fast. I was scared. This time, I didn't care if my dad knew it.

Dad opened the door and entered the room slowly. He looked around. First, he went to the dresser and peeked behind it. Nothing. Then he bent down and looked under the bed. Nothing.

Finally, he walked over to the closet. He paused and looked at me. I didn't want to see what might be hiding among my clothes. He yanked on the door.

Something from the top shelf came flying straight for his head. He moved quickly out of the way. It passed his head and hit the floor.

"Oh no, the attack of the killer baseball glove," he said, laughing.

I walked into the room and looked around myself. I

spun around to face him. "Dad, I'm telling you, I saw something." Suddenly, I felt a soft, thin ghostly material rush up my back and brush the side of my face. A shiver hit my spine and raced to my head. I jumped up and landed right on the bed. My heart was beating so hard that I thought someone could see it through my shirt.

"Okay, Buddy, I think I see what the problem is. Your window is open. Maybe a bird got in. Just a second ago the wind blew the curtain. It touched you and you nearly hit the ceiling! I think you better lay off the pizza with extra cheese for a while. Your imagination is a little too active."

Dad tousled my hair before he walked out the door.

I felt like a little kid. Dad was right. I was letting my imagination run wild. I decided to ignore my eerie feelings and the stories about the witch. After all, I was almost a teenager. I was too old to be acting like a little kid.

When I had finished putting away my books I decided to lie down for a few minutes. I was still tired from all the unpacking I'd done. I got comfortable and closed my eyes. I began to softly drift to sleep.

All of a sudden I felt something press against my head. Whatever it was pressed harder, until it became difficult for me to breathe.

I felt as if someone was pressing a pillow on my head. The thought jolted me.

Something was trying to smother me!

27

When I opened my eyes I saw that Snowball was lying on my head again. Apparently I had fallen asleep and had not felt him jump up on the bed.

I moved his warm, furry body off the bed and onto the floor.

I rolled over on my side, closed my eyes, and tried to rest again. But the scare had jolted me and I could not shut off my mind. I got up and walked downstairs.

I looked at the clock on the kitchen wall. It was already four o'clock. I had slept for almost two hours.

I was opening the refrigerator to get something to drink when Dad walked into the kitchen.

"Well, I see Rip Van Winkle has awakened from his sleep."

"Huh?" Dad had caught me off guard.

"I peeked in on you earlier. You were out like a light."

"Oh. Well, I got my books put away. But then I decided to rest for a while, and you know, I guess I fell asleep."

"You don't have to explain, Buddy." Dad put his hand on my shoulder. "Moving is tiring business."

Dad turned to walk out of the kitchen, but he stopped abruptly. "Say, we've still got to get those mousetraps. Want to ride to the store with me?"

I had forgotten about the mousetraps too, though I had not forgotten the experience in the basement the day before. I wasn't convinced that what Snowball had seen down there was a mouse.

"Sure, Dad."

Dad went upstairs to ask Mom if she needed anything from the store.

When he came back downstairs I was waiting for him outside the garage. The garage was still packed with boxes so he couldn't park his car in there.

Dad and I got into the car.

"Your Mom's busy rigging up her computer. She'll probably have it up and running by the time we get back." Dad started the ignition and began to back out of the driveway.

My mom was a freelance writer. Ever since I could remember she had an office in our home.

Dad and I didn't talk much on the way to the store. Both of us were busy looking at the sights of our new hometown.

The store clerk helped us find the mousetraps. Dad bought a half dozen of them. He explained to me that if you see one mouse in the house, that probably means you have several of them.

29

On the way back home, Dad stopped to buy us both an ice-cream cone. Again, we were silent on the ride home. But this time it was because we were busy licking our ice cream.

As Dad pulled into our driveway I looked at the front of our house. My room was on the left side of the house facing the front. When I looked up at the window of my room, I saw something move.

I fixed my eyes on the window. Sure enough, I saw the outline of a figure standing there. The window was too far away for me to see the figure clearly. But there was definitely something there.

I couldn't speak. I couldn't even tell Dad to look up. I was too frightened. I sat there staring at the figure through tree limbs.

Finally, my voice broke through and with a crackling, high-pitched tone I yelled to Dad while pointing to my room. "Dad, look. There's something in my window."

Just as he tilted his head to look up, the figure disappeared.

Dad and I walked into the house just as Mom was walking out of the family room.

"Hi, guys. Did you get the traps?"

"Sure did," Dad replied. "All we have to do now is set them out in the basement."

"Max, what's wrong? You look like you've seen a ghost." Mom stepped closer to me.

"I saw something . . . something standing near the window in my room." I was still shaken.

"Did you see it just a few minutes ago? When you and your dad pulled into the driveway?" I thought I detected a smile coming across my mother's face as she spoke.

"Yes! Exactly. How did you know?"

"Because that was me you saw. I was trying to close your bedroom window when you two pulled up. But it's stuck. It's the same with the sewing room window. There's no screen on those windows and I don't want the flies to get in. See if you can close them before you go to bed tonight, okay?" Mom smiled at me.

I felt myself flush with embarrassment. Once again, my imagination had made me look silly.

Mom and Dad must have sensed my embarrassment because neither of them said any more about it.

I was about to excuse myself and go up to my room when I heard a loud noise.

"What was that?" Dad asked.

Though the noise had scared me, I was relieved that someone else had heard it, too. I was afraid it was my imagination again.

"It sounded like it came from the family room," Mom said. "Oh, no! I just put Tommy in there!"

The three of us raced toward the family room, with Mom in the lead.

When we got there Tommy was standing at the side of his playpen. He grinned widely and began to chatter away in an unidentifiable language.

Dad picked up Tommy. Mom looked around to see what could have made the noise.

Mom spotted Tommy's rattle on the floor. She reached down and picked it up. "Well, it looks like our Tommy has a pretty good pitching arm. I think what we heard was this rattle hitting the wall."

Tommy let out a wail of glee as though he understood Mom was talking about him. Everyone laughed.

That night after dinner, Mom and Dad said they were tired.

"We can finish the unpacking tomorrow," Dad said.

He was taking Monday off, but he had to be back at work Tuesday morning.

"Sounds good to me," Mom said. "I'm beat."

I wasn't sleepy, though. I was still rested from my long afternoon nap.

"I think I'll stay up a while and watch TV. I'm really not very tired," I said.

"Okay. You did sleep a long time this afternoon." Dad paused long enough to yawn. "But don't stay up late. We've got another busy day tomorrow."

"All right, Dad. Goodnight, Mom."

"Goodnight, Max." Now it was Mom's turn to yawn.

Mom and Dad walked upstairs to their bedroom. I went to the kitchen and grabbed the last slice of pizza with extra cheese. Snowball was at my feet. He liked pizza, too. I usually let him have the edges of the crust that I didn't eat.

I brought the pizza back to the family room and sat down on the sofa. I had the remote control in one hand. The slice of pizza with extra cheese was in the other hand. My faithful dog was next to me with his eye on the slice of pizza.

I flipped through the channels until I found a movie that looked pretty interesting. I sat back and watched the movie while I finished off the slice of pizza. I gave the edge of the crust to Snowball. He took it and trotted out of the room.

The movie was about this alien that would grab people and pull them into a hole. The victims got wrapped up like flies in a spiderweb. He came back later and ate them. After about an hour I began to get bored with the movie. I felt my eyelids getting heavier.

My eyes closed and I forced them open. This happened several times. My eyelids felt like they weighed a ton. They closed again. But this time when I opened them two space aliens were on the TV screen talking to me. It was happening again.

"You are ours. You can't escape us. We have come to take you. No power is greater than we are," they spoke right to me. I saw their beady, red eyes peering out of the screen as if they were alive and real and in the room with me.

"We want you. We want you to join us in our world. We have come to get you and take you back to our world," the aliens said.

The aliens had long black ears that stuck up in the air alongside their tiny yellow horns. Their eyebrows curved upward. Their red eyes blazed like night-lights in a dark room. Their noses were hooked and pointed down at their twisted, grinning mouths.

Out of the mouths came long, pointed fangs that dripped fresh blood. I watched as the blood dripped down their chins and then fell. They were creepy enough to look at, but the dripping blood was what truly frightened me.

I watched as each drop came off the fang and hit the frame of the TV. My jaw dropped open when I saw that first drop hit the frame and drip outside of it and onto the floor. It was starting to look bad for me.

One of the aliens started to crawl out of the set. His long bony fingers grabbed the side of the set like it was a window frame. His nails scraped across the wood cabinet, leaving deep gashes in the grain. The scraping sounded like a screeching bird.

He pulled his body through the TV screen. When his first leg swung out of the television, I noticed that the foot was long and thin. With its long and pointed nails the foot looked like that of a wild animal. He started stepping toward me.

The other alien was right behind him. He was grinning and his big upper teeth hung below his lip. I was sure that I also saw blood dripping from the long pointed fangs.

They moved toward me. One to my left and one to my right. The aliens approached me with their long hands outstretched. It looked like it was the end for me.

I tried to run, but my body was frozen on the couch. It felt like I was caught in a web.

The aliens stood in front of me. Their eyes looked thirsty for my blood.

The first alien reached for my left arm. The other grabbed the right arm. They pulled me off the sofa and I dropped onto the floor. I tried to scream, but all the air was being sucked from my lungs.

They pulled me across the floor toward the TV. My

legs scraped along the carpet. I felt the carpet pile dig into them. I wanted to twist away, but I couldn't fight. I couldn't scream. This was the end, I knew it.

One of them got under me and the other went back inside the TV. The one inside pulled my arms into the screen. I passed right through it as if it wasn't there. The other pushed me from underneath. I was halfway in. My feet and legs hung out of the front of the TV and the rest of my body was inside the set. In another few seconds I'd be another face on a milk carton. I had to do something.

Finally I felt a puff of air come into my lungs and I screamed.

I felt the presence of something else in the room. Something very large and powerful. It grabbed me by the shoulders.

11

"Max, wake up. You're having a nightmare." Dad was shaking me as he called out my name. I looked up at him. He had no idea how glad I was to see him.

"Dad, it was so real. I really thought I was being pulled inside the TV by two aliens. They were going to eat me or something." I was talking quickly.

He smiled at me. "You better get up to bed, son," he said. "Lay off the pizza for a while. I think your aliens are caused by tomato sauce and extra cheese."

I headed upstairs with Dad right behind me. I was really tired now. All I wanted to do was sleep. Dad stopped me before I got to my room.

"Buddy, do you think this move has been too hard on you?" Dad asked.

"What do you mean?" I wondered.

"Well, you've been having these dreams and seeing things."

"I'm okay, Dad. You're probably right that it's too much pizza or something like that. I'll get a good

37

night's sleep, and tomorrow things should be fine," I told him.

Dad hugged me and I went into my room. I was out the moment my head hit the pillow, but my mind didn't shut off. My dreams were wild and frightening.

In one of them, the alien crept into my bedroom and walked across me. I dreamed that I looked up and saw another set of eyes, but they were yellow ones. The dream was so real that I awoke and sat straight up in my bed.

I was sure that I felt something leap off me and scurry across the room. But then again, I had been sure that the other things I had imagined were real as well. I laid my head back down. It must have been a dream, nothing more. That was what I thought.

12

We spent all day Monday unpacking. By late afternoon we had finished. I had been so busy that I didn't have time to imagine any space aliens or other haunting figures.

Keith called to say he would pick me up for the youth meeting so Dad wouldn't have to drive me there. He said we were going to eat dinner at an old train station that had been converted into a restaurant. I was excited.

Keith was right on time. He had already picked up the others. I piled into the backseat with Eve and Jamal. Aaron sat up front with Keith. The two of them talked about basketball during the ride to the restaurant. Eve brought up the subject of baseball. As it turned out, she was a Cubs fan like Mom and Dad. She, Jamal, and I discussed the highlights of last Saturday's game.

The restaurant was as neat as Keith said it would be. We were seated in one of the old train cars.

The restaurant specialized in burgers—all different kinds. I, of course, ordered a pizza burger.

As we ate our dinner, Eve asked me if I had seen anything unusual in the witch house. I wasn't sure if I should say anything. They might have thought I was nuts. So, instead I asked her to tell me more about why it was called the witch house.

Aaron spoke first. "Some kids disappeared in the woods behind the house."

"I already told him that one," Jamal said. "My cousin says he knows somebody that actually saw the old woman fly out her back window on a broom."

Eve laughed and said, "She used to wear all black. She had long, black hair. I bumped into her once at the grocery store. She had her cart filled with cat food."

"And eye of newt," Jamal joked.

"Some strange things have happened since we moved in," I said. I felt that I could open up now.

Jamal got excited. "Cool, like what?"

I told them about my experience in the coal cellar.

"So you don't think what your dog saw was a mouse?" Aaron asked.

"I'm not sure. Like I said, I never got a look at it."

"There's no telling what was, or is, in your basement," Jamal said.

"I've never been in the witch house before," Eve said.

"Me either," said Jamal.

"That makes three of us," Aaron added.

40

So I invited Jamal, Eve, and Aaron to come to my house the next day.

Jamal jumped at the chance to search the witch house. Aaron seemed a little hesitant. But when Eve said she wanted to check it out, Aaron decided he could make it, too.

On the ride home from the restaurant, we agreed on a time to meet the next day.

When we pulled up to the front of my house, Jamal screamed and grabbed Aaron's arm. Keith and Aaron spun around in their seats to look at Jamal. "What's wrong?" Aaron gasped.

Jamal pointed to one of the upstairs windows—the window to my bedroom.

My pulse began to race.

13

Jamal laughed. "Got ya," he said.

Eve grinned.

"Sorry, guys. I was just fooling around," Jamal said meekly.

Aaron stared blankly at Jamal for a moment, then he smiled. "That was a good one," he said, and he began to chuckle.

Aaron's chuckle erupted into laughter. That set off a chain reaction, and soon everyone in the car was laughing.

Finally, I said goodnight to everyone and stepped out of the car. I stood on the sidewalk and waved good-bye as the car pulled away from the curb.

After watching TV for an hour, I went to bed.

Later, I woke up when Snowball licked my face. I looked at the clock. It was two in the morning. I turned over to go back to sleep. That's when I heard a sound coming from the room next to me. It sounded like a moan.

I thought it was Tommy crying. I pulled the covers off me to go see what the problem was.

I listened again. The moaning wasn't coming from Tommy's room. It came from the room on the other side of me. That room was going to be the sewing room. There was nothing but boxes in it. There was nothing there that would moan.

I had to see what was in the room. I slipped carefully out of my bed. My feet touched the cool floor. My heart was beating hard.

I opened my door quietly. The hallway was dark. The night-light wasn't on. It was a bad night for it to be off.

I felt my way down the hall to the spare room. It was so dark that I had to inch my way. Each step felt like it took a minute. As I got closer to the door, the moaning got louder.

I twisted the doorknob easily. Every door in this old house creaked. So if I wanted to surprise whoever was in there, I needed to push the door open fast.

I flung the door open. A dark figure was standing in the window frame. The moaning stopped. The figure turned around quickly and looked at me. Its yellow eyes stared at me. I was frozen with fear.

The figure leaped at me. I covered my face and jumped back. Something was behind me on the floor. I fell over it and hit the hallway floor hard.

The figure flew by me and hissed. I heard its long claws scrape across the hallway floor and then down

43

the stairs. I couldn't see it anymore in the darkness, but I was sure it looked like the beings in my dream.

Mom peeked out her door. "What happened, Max?" she asked.

I didn't want to tell her what I just saw. She would think I was imagining it. I called back in a whisper, "I thought I heard Tommy crying so I got up to check the room and I guess I tripped."

"Are you both all right?" she asked.

"Just fine, Mom. Go ahead and go back to bed," I answered.

"Okay, you get back to bed, too. Have sweet dreams, honey," she said.

"I will, Mom, but I'm a little thirsty. I'm going downstairs to get a drink of water," I told her.

"It's probably because of all the pizza that you've been eating," she said as she closed her door.

Sweet dreams after what I just saw would be a little difficult.

I walked downstairs. I wanted to get a drink, that was true. But I also wanted to see where the creature may have gone.

The living room was empty when I looked in it. I heard nothing and saw nothing. I moved into the dining room and checked under the table and found nothing again. The kitchen was next.

I was walking toward it when I passed the basement door. I bet it was hiding in the basement. I put my ear to the door and listened. I heard nothing.

I decided that I had to open the door to check further. I could not leave a creature running around our house. I had a little brother to protect. I also had a dog to protect because obviously he was not going to protect me.

My hand gripped the doorknob. This time I was looking for the creature and not waiting for it to come after me. I surprised myself at how bold I was getting. I popped the door open and stuck my head into the dark stairway and listened. I heard nothing.

It seemed to me that the creature must have left the house. I did not know how it traveled or how it moved. I only knew that I saw the beast upstairs and it went downstairs. I could not find it downstairs, so it must have left by some means that I didn't know.

Since the creature was gone, I thought that I would pour a glass of water and then go back to bed. I walked into the kitchen and headed for the cupboard.

As I reached up for a glass I heard a noise in the corner by the sink. It was too dark to see what it was. I froze and said, "Who is it?" That was not a particularly brilliant thing to say, but I was scared and that was the first thing I could think of.

My voice must have frightened the creature. Suddenly I felt the sharp claws of my attacker across my bare feet. I jumped for safety on top of the kitchen counter and heard the sharp claws race across the tile floor.

I spun around. In the dark all I could see was a black

form leaping through the doorway to the basement. I forgot about my drink of water and ran for the staircase to the upstairs. I took the steps three at a time until I hit the top.

"Sweet dreams," my mom had said. Forget it. Any dream that I had at that point would not be sweet. I went into my room and turned on my bedside light.

Then I heard the moaning again. This time, it was coming up through the ductwork from the basement. This time, I wasn't going to go see what it was. This time, I just pulled the covers over my head and started to pray.

When morning came, Dad was waiting for a cab to take him to the airport. He had to go on a two-day trip.

I wanted to ask Dad if he had heard the moaning sound last night. If maybe he thought there might be something else in this house besides mice. But obviously he and Mom hadn't heard anything last night or they would have said something about it.

The taxi arrived and I hugged Dad good-bye.

I straightened my room up as I waited for Jamal, Aaron, and Eve to come over. I thought we would have a great time. I had not explored the woods behind the house yet. I thought that would be a fun thing for us to do today.

Aaron arrived first. He and Mom hit it off great. He helped Mom and me make chocolate chip cookies as we waited for Jamal and Eve. I kept sticking my finger in the dough. I like the raw dough almost as much as the baked cookies themselves.

When Eve and Jamal arrived, we set out for the woods. We found one tree that was worthy of a tree house. We all talked about building one in it. Of course, we'd get cable, a big-screen TV, a microwave, and a small refrigerator to go inside the tree house.

When we went in the house, Jamal leaned over and whispered, "Can we see the basement now?"

We headed down the stairs with Snowball at our heels.

I told the story about how the creature had come rushing out of the coal cellar right at me. I told them that I had spun around and tried to grab it. It was too fast for me to catch, but my actions definitely scared it away. Aaron wasn't sure he wanted to enter the coal cellar.

As we walked toward the open doorway we heard a scratching noise coming from inside.

"I'm not sure this is such a good idea," Aaron said.

Jamal shot back, "But we need to know what's in there."

Jamal took a few steps closer and stopped dead in his tracks. "Whatever was scratching inside is coming toward us," he said as he jumped back.

I gulped.

15

We all stood silently watching the doorway.

Snowball came out of the coal cellar. We all let out a sigh of relief, and then we started laughing.

"Come, Snowball," I called. He walked over to me. His muzzle and front paws were covered with dirt. "He's been digging in there," I said.

"Come on. Let's check it out," Jamal said as he hurried inside the coal cellar.

By the time I got inside the cellar, Jamal was kneeling beside a hole dug in the dirt floor. Eve followed closely behind me. Aaron waited in the doorway.

"Turn on the light, Max. It's hard to see in here," he said.

I pulled the string to the light switch. The light didn't come on.

"I forgot. The lightbulb is dead," I said.

"Aaron, step out of the doorway," Jamal said. "You're blocking the light from the basement."

Aaron stepped inside the cellar and walked to where Eve and I now stood behind Jamal.

"What do you suppose Snowball was digging for?" Eve asked.

"I don't know," I answered. "Maybe he was digging for a mouse."

"Or maybe he was digging for bones," Aaron said. "Bones that the witch buried down here."

I stiffened. What if Aaron was right? Jamal had said that bones were found in the woods behind the house. Maybe the witch had buried bones here, too—where no one could find them.

"Jamal, do you see anything?" Eve asked.

He didn't answer.

"Jamal?" Eve shook his shoulder.

Jamal stood up slowly. The light from the doorway shone on him. His face had lost its expression. His eyes were blank. He started walking toward us like a zombie. We all took a step back. Eve grabbed me and Aaron grabbed Eve.

Jamal spoke in a low, spooky voice, "You have trespassed on my property. You have uncovered my secret burial site. Your fate is in my hands."

Eve and I screamed in unison. Aaron was shaking.

I looked at Jamal. He took another step closer. His arms were raised and his hands open.

Eve, Aaron, and I took another step backward. Jamal started laughing.

"Got ya, again," he said.

Eve groaned.

Aaron looked at Jamal and said, "I knew it all the time. I knew you were faking."

"No, you didn't." Jamal laughed.

"Let's get out of here," Aaron said. "This exploring stuff isn't much fun anymore."

I agreed with Aaron. "How about some video games?" I asked.

We headed upstairs to the family room.

Mom had put out a plate of cookies for us.

What I saw when I walked into the family room made me lose my appetite.

In the middle of the cookie plate was Snowball. The brown chocolate chips were gooey across his white beard and mustache.

"Snowball, get down!" I commanded. My gruff command frightened him and he scurried out of the room.

"Well, so much for the cookies," Jamal said. "Have you found any other scary things in the witch house?"

"Yeah. I haven't thought of this since it happened. On the day I first saw something in the basement, I also explored the attic. I heard a noise up there. It turned out to be nothing but the wind whistling through a broken window."

"Did you see anything up there?" Jamal asked.

"There were these old trunks. I wanted to see what was inside them, but I didn't have enough time then. I bet there is a map to a pirate's treasure in one of them," I told them.

"What are we waiting for? I want to see what's up there," Eve said.

We headed up the front staircase to the second floor

and down the hall to the attic door. As I reached the top, Jamal pushed past me and into the attic.

"Hey, who brought the flashlight?" he asked.

Eve looked at him strangely. "Why?" she asked.

"If we are going to look inside a dark trunk in a dark attic, we need light," Jamal said.

"Let there be light," Eve said as she reached up to pull the string attached to the light. Before she could pull the string we were startled by a scream.

"What is it?" Jamal yelled to the screaming Aaron.

"It's a person. There's a person up here," he said with fright in his voice.

"It isn't a person," I said. "Eve, turn on the light so everyone can see what it is."

She gave the string a quick tug.

"I forgot to tell you all that this was up here. It scared me the first time I saw it. In the dark it's really hard to know exactly what it is. But as you can see in the light it's nothing more than a sewing model."

"Since Eve has so kindly ended our light crisis, I think we should dig into those trunks," Jamal said.

I tried to open the biggest one first. It was locked. I went to the smaller one and it was locked also. "They're both locked. Anybody here a locksmith when they're not in school?"

Aaron walked over to the trunk and looked at it. "I think I can get it open. I've been reading some books on magic. The great magicians were always excellent lock pickers. I've learned a few things."

Aaron pulled a little penknife from his pocket and stuck the point inside the lock. It popped open.

"I guess if middle school doesn't work out for you then you can get a job as a cat burglar," Eve said.

Aaron laughed at that and said, "Why would I want to steal cats?"

Eve thumped him on the head and laughed. Then she flipped open the top of the trunk. On top were a bunch of old newspapers. She pulled them out and handed the stack to me.

"Wow! I can't believe we are holding something this old," I said. "The date on these papers is 1917. The headlines are about a war. That would be World War I!"

Aaron grabbed for the stack. "Let's see the sports page," he said.

As he pulled the stack out of my hands the old paper started to crumble. "Wow," Aaron said. "The paper is dry and brittle. It crumbles if you handle it too roughly. This is history."

Eve and I dug deeper into the trunk. We pulled out some old clothing and photographs. Near the bottom was a cardboard gift box that was tied with a string. Eve pulled it out gently. Untying the string, she lifted the top off the box.

I screamed and Eve dropped the box.

Inside the box was a green glass ball. It had an eerie glow to it.

"It's just a piece of glass," Eve said.

"A *strange* piece of glass," I added.

"You never know what you'll find in the witch house. I'll get it out of there," she said as her hands dipped back into the trunk and pulled out the glowing, green glass orb. She handed it to me.

I started turning it around and around to see if there were any markings on it. As I spun it, the ball started glowing brighter. The inside of the ball appeared to soften and turn to a liquid.

"Hey, look at this. The inside of the ball is changing," I called to the other three. Eve was still kneeling at the trunk and Jamal was rummaging through the remaining contents. Aaron stepped up behind me. As I held it, the liquid began to bubble.

"Can I see it?" Aaron reached up for the ball.

"This is really cool. Well, not actually cool like cold

because I'm starting to feel it warm up. Look, it's bubbling. It looks like it is actually boiling."

Aaron was smiling at the glowing ball bubbling in his hand. It started to vibrate a little. He smiled some more and looked at Eve. "Hey, this thing is starting to move. You hold it for a while. The more it bubbles the more it vibrates."

Aaron reached out with the ball in his hands and gave it to Eve. She stared at it and turned the orb over and over watching it bubble. "This is really cool," she said. The ball continued bubbling and then letters came floating to the glass surface. "Look at this," she shouted. "Letters are appearing."

Eve's last remark got Jamal's attention. He stopped rummaging through the trunk. "Hey, let me take a look at that thing," he said.

Jamal walked over to Eve's side and watched as she continued to turn the glass ball over. "I know what this is," he said, "and it's very valuable."

"Valuable? What do you mean?" Eve asked.

"It's very old. My grandmother and I saw one in an antique store once. The shopkeeper said it was a children's game."

"So how do you play it?" Aaron asked.

"You ask a question, then you spin the ball around until the letters bubble to the top. The letters spell out an answer. It's kind of like a Magic Eight Ball."

Eve stopped spinning the ball. "Okay. Let me ask it

a question. Magic Ball, is my family going to the beach for summer vacation?"

Eve rapidly turned the ball around until the letters began to rise to the top. The letter *N* surfaced first, followed by the letter *O*.

"Sorry about that, Eve," Jamal said. "It looks like the answer is 'No.'"

"But that's the right answer. We're not going to the beach. We're going to the mountains this year."

"Let me try," I said, taking the ball from Eve. "Magic Ball, do I live in a witch house?"

The letters bubbled to the top: *Y-E-S*.

I was so shaken that I dropped the ball and it fell into the trunk. Before I could pick it up again, the lid to the trunk fell shut. We heard the lock snap into place.

18

"Max, why did you do that?" Eve asked. "What did it say?"

"Never mind. It's no big deal," I answered. Although I didn't believe in the Magic Ball, I was still a little shaky.

"But I want to ask the Magic Ball a question," Jamal said.

Jamal tried to open the lid of the trunk, but it was locked again. Eve tried, but to no avail. It was definitely locked. She looked at Aaron and asked, "Hey, cat burglar, do you want to try out your stuff one more time?"

Aaron knelt down next to the trunk and pulled out his pocketknife. He inserted the blade and moved it up and down and in and out. But the lock would not give up the fight. "I can't get it open," he finally said.

"Now what?" I asked.

"Do we have any other ideas? It looks like we are not going to play the Magic Ball game anymore," Eve said.

"We could look in the other trunk. Let me try to pick that lock," Aaron said. He moved to the smaller trunk and inserted his knife. It popped right open. "I thought you said that this one was locked."

"I did. I was sure it was locked. Maybe it was just stuck and you loosened it," I responded.

"Well, it's open now. Who would like to do the honors?" Aaron asked.

"I'll try again." Eve placed her hands on the lid and started to raise it when a high-pitched voice called from behind her, "Do not open that trunk!"

Eve jumped and spun around. Aaron plastered his body against the bare wall. I reached for something to use to defend us. We all turned in unison to see Jamal's smiling face.

"Got you again," Jamal said through his laugh.

"Jamal, I'm getting a little nervous in this house as it is. Don't make it any worse," Aaron said.

"All right. I get the point. I'm sorry. So let's take a look at what's in the other trunk," Jamal said apologetically.

Eve reached down to open the trunk. I put my hand on top of it to stop her. "What if there is something like a skeleton in there? Or it could be where the creature stays. The witch could have kept her stuff for spells in there. Maybe we should not open it," I told them.

"It could also be that treasure map you were talking

about. This could be our chance to be rich and famous," Jamal said.

"If it is a map to pirate treasure then I'm going to take my share and buy a moped," Aaron told us.

Eve laughed and spoke up. "If this is pirate treasure then you could buy more than a moped."

"Then I'll buy two mopeds," Aaron joked.

Eve put her hands on the lid one more time and started to ease it up when we heard a noise coming from the other side of the attic. Then there was a loud crash, and we were plunged into darkness.

"Ouch!" Jamal cried out.

"Are you okay, Jamal?" I yelled.

"No. When I heard that noise I snapped to a standing position, but I was right under the lightbulb. My head smashed it," he answered. "I'm not bleeding, so I guess I'm all right. But what made that noise?"

Aaron whispered, "It came from over there." He pointed to the window. "I can't see anything though."

I felt around in the dark for the piece of wood. It would be the second time I needed it in my own attic. "Stay close to me. I have a weapon."

We inched across the dark floor. The sun was starting to go down, and the light was getting grayer by the second. I rounded the corner first, followed by Eve, then Aaron. I wasn't sure where Jamal had gone.

I turned to Eve and Aaron and whispered, "The window is right around this next corner. Be ready for anything."

We took another step. I had my eyes closed. I was

afraid of what might be there. Eve's poke into my back made me open them rapidly.

"Do you see anything?" she asked.

I looked. There was something lurking in the shadows near the window. I could not make out the figure in the dark corner. But I saw the glow of its eyes. The two yellow eyes were unmistakable.

"It's the creature!" I yelled. I turned around to look for my friends.

By the time I turned my head back around the beast was nothing but a dark shape flying out the window.

The others had gotten around the corner too late to see it. No one would believe me.

"Where's the creature, Max?" Eve asked.

"He just jumped out the window," I answered.

Jamal pushed his way past the others. He looked directly at me. "I believe you, Max. There is something here in this house, and we all heard the noise. We may have missed it this time, but we won't next time."

Jamal turned to look at Eve and Aaron. "Don't you think that it's strange that the moment we prepare to open the smaller trunk, the creature appears? Have you thought about why Max found it locked and then Aaron discovered it unlocked? All this is starting to add up to something out of a horror movie. If we were smart, we would run to the police."

"Yeah, but the police won't believe us without any evidence," Aaron said.

"You have a point there, Aaron. My suggestion is that we open that trunk to see what's inside it. Any takers on that idea?" Jamal said to us.

"Don't we need light to see inside it?" Eve asked.

"We'll drag it over by the window," I said.

We dragged the trunk toward the window. Once it was there, Eve tried again to lift the lid. This time the lock seemed jammed.

"The lock won't open," she said.

"Just like I said, the creature doesn't want us to open the trunk. Aaron, your job is to get us deeper into trouble by opening that big box," Jamal directed.

Aaron had the lock opened in a few seconds. Eve popped open the lid. We expected something to fly out at us. Nothing came out.

But the item on top of the junk inside shocked us.

20

"It's a map!" Eve said excitedly.

"I told you that there was probably a map inside," Jamal shouted.

Eve pulled it out and took it to the window for a closer look. We followed her.

The map was drawn inside a square. It started with a dot that said "here" next to it. From that dot a straight line continued. Next to the line was written "ten S-T." The line took a right turn and went into an area marked "B and R." Once in the B and R area, the line went left and passed through what looked like an archway. Then the line came to a dead stop at a spot called Richland.

"This map ought to take us right to the pirate's treasure. We have found what we came for. Now we know why the creature tried to stop us. It must have been sent here by the witch to protect the treasure," Aaron said.

I was getting excited. "I only have one question. Where does the spot here begin?"

"It could begin where we found the trunk," Jamal suggested.

"That's impossible. A person can't take ten steps from the trunk. You will run into a wall," Eve reminded us.

"Then it must begin at the bottom of the stairway where the attic door is," I ventured.

Eve said, "Max is right. Let's go down there and begin our search for pirate's gold."

We descended the staircase. Eve stood right behind me. "Take the ten steps. Hurry!" she said.

I paced off ten steps. I was standing directly in front of the spare bedroom. I looked at the others. "I heard the creature in here before. It may be waiting behind this door. Who wants to go first?"

The three of them backed away from me. Aaron said, "We're just guests in this house. I think the host should lead his people to the promised 'Richland.'"

Eve and Jamal agreed with him entirely too fast for my liking. They were right, I supposed. It was my house.

I twisted the knob and slowly pressed open the door. No lights were on and the sun had just gone down. It was too dark to see if it was even in there.

"Turn on the light," Aaron whispered from behind me.

"The only light is on the dresser on the other side of the room," I answered.

"Go turn it on or we won't be able to find the pirate's treasure," he insisted.

I entered the room. Each step filled me with fear. *What if the creature is in here?* I asked myself. *What if it grabs me?*

I moved on my tiptoes so I would not disturb any sleeping beast from beyond. I was close to the light. When I reached out to grab it something pulled my arm away.

21

I stifled a scream. I twisted my head to see what had grabbed me.

Eve stood behind me. "Don't do it!" she said with a whisper. "If someone outside on the street is watching us through the window, they will see where the treasure is. We will have to do this in the dark."

"How?" I asked.

"On the map it looks like we are to turn about halfway in the B and R, or bedroom as we now know. That would put the arches inside that closet. Do you know what is on the other side of that closet?" Eve was thinking things through very carefully.

"As far as I know, the garage is on that side of the house. I imagine a wall is right there where the arches are drawn," I told her.

"Then we need to go into that closet," she said.

I didn't know what my parents had put inside the closet in the spare bedroom, but I was about to find out. Jamal and Aaron stood close to me as I opened the door to the closet. We all braced ourselves in case something flew out at us, but nothing did.

The family's winter coats were hanging in the closet. As I stepped into the closet to see what was on the other side, I thought of The Chronicles of Narnia and how the kids in the story stepped into a wardrobe closet. They passed through furry coats as well. But after they entered the closet they stepped into a mystical world.

This was a lot like that experience. Only when I got to the back of the closet, I did not enter some mystical wintry world. Instead, I smashed my nose against a hard plaster wall.

"That's it. A wall is here," I called back to the others.

Eve pushed her way in through the coats. She was grasping around for something in the air. After she found what she was looking for, she told Aaron and Jamal to get inside the closet and to close the door.

As soon as Jamal closed the door we heard him say, "Oops!"

"What happened, Jamal?" Aaron asked.

"I just forgot to check to see if the door was locked," he said timidly. He turned the doorknob. "Okay. It's unlocked. We're safe inside this closet with our protectors, the great furry coat army."

Eve yanked the pull chain, turning on the light. "It should be safe. No one will know we are looking for anything because they could not see this light. Everybody should search for some kind of secret panel."

"That's ridiculous. This is not some weird house," I protested.

"It's not?" Jamal shot back.

"I get your point," I said.

We looked around for a hidden panel for a long time. We all were getting nervous. Aaron and Jamal started to horse around.

Just as they slammed their weight against the back wall, part of it popped open.

22

We smelled a heavy, musty odor. That door had not been opened in years. When it opened it sent dust flying into the closet. It was like a fog had rolled over us. The dust particles seemed to dance in the light. I've always loved watching dust drift along in a sunbeam. This was like that, only a thousand times more.

Once the dust cleared we peered through the doorway. The room beyond the door must have been built over the garage. The shelves inside the room were designed into the open-beamed, slanted roofline. Some old empty jars sat on the shelves.

We ventured inside the room. The floor creaked with each step we took. Eve went to the left and looked along those shelves, and Aaron went to the right. Jamal and I stood guard in the opening.

Aaron whispered to us, "I can't find a thing except for dust and more dust. From the looks of things, whatever was stored up here was taken out years ago."

"Aaron, could you carbon-date the dust for us?" Jamal joked.

"Real funny. But then again, who's the A student in science?" Aaron retorted.

Eve moved around the corner out of our sight. I called to her, "Eve, where are you?"

"I'm back here. I think I see something in the corner. Come help me drag it into the light," she said.

Aaron and I went to help Eve while Jamal guarded the door.

When we got to Eve she was crouched down in the corner. As we got closer, I saw her face. Her eyes were closed, her mouth was wide open, and her tongue was hanging out.

I ran the last few steps toward her. When I reached down to help her I expected to find the worst. As I grabbed her shoulders, her two hands shot up and grabbed me by the arms.

"Ah!" I screamed. I fell over backward.

"Just joking, Max," Eve apologized as she pulled me to my feet.

"That's all right. I'm getting used to being scared around this house. Tell us what you found besides my heart that leaped out of my mouth," I told her.

"I found another trunk," she said.

Aaron asked, "Do you think that the treasure is inside?"

"Once we drag it into the light, we will open it and

find out. Help me get it back to the closet door," Eve directed.

The trunk was heavy, but the anticipation kept us moving it along. We slid it into the best light that broke into the secret room from the secret passage in the mysterious closet.

The trunk wasn't locked, but it had been tied with a cord. Our excitement grew as Aaron pulled his knife from his pocket and cut the cord.

I took a deep breath and grabbed the lid. "Friends, this is it. Inside this trunk is going to be enough pirate's gold for us to buy whatever we want."

"Maybe I'll buy *three* mopeds," Aaron joked.

I chuckled then sucked in a breath. It was the moment of truth. I lifted the lid and tossed it back.

"What's in there?" Eve yelled.

I reached my hand inside and pulled out a bunch of chains. "Nothing but chains," I said.

Aaron grabbed one of the chains and inspected it. "They're tire chains," he said. "People once put them on their car tires in the winter. You know, for better traction."

"Thank you, Dr. Gadget," I kidded. "Let's get out of here. I think we just went on another wild rabbit trail."

We looked up just as the closet door was swinging shut. We heard the lock click. We were locked in the secret room in the midst of solid darkness.

23

"What do we do now?" Eve asked.

"Scream for help," Jamal said.

"No, we can't do that. My mom and dad already think that I have this weird imagination. They say it's caused by eating pizza with extra cheese. All they need is one more crazy thing to add to their list, and then my pizza-eating days are over. I'd rather stay here and rot than have my pizza supply cut off," I told them.

"If I'm not home soon, I'll have my head cut off," Jamal said. "We need to get out of here now!"

"Do not fear, Dr. Gadget is here. I think I see a way out of this place," Aaron told us.

"If you can show us the way to get out of here, then do it," Eve said.

"If you study the dancing dust mites, you will see that there is a square-shaped box of light in that back corner. That, my friends, is coming from the trapdoor to the garage. All we need to do is pry it open and drop down through the opening to our freedom."

"Absolutely brilliant, Holmes. How do you do it?" I joked.

"Elementary, my dear Watson, elementary," he answered.

Jamal was snickering as he walked over to us. "Okay, Sherlock Holmes and Doctor Watson, would you please help us pry open this trapdoor?"

"Why?" Eve asked. "We just have to pull it up with this rope." She tugged on the rope and the trapdoor opened.

I stuck my head inside the garage. I rolled over and looked up at my friends and said, "I've got some good news and some bad news. The good news is that I'm glad I forgot to turn the light off in the garage today. The bad news is that we have to drop ten feet into a bunch of empty boxes. They should break our fall so that we don't break any bones."

"Anything to get out of here," Jamal said as he slipped through the opening and fell to the boxes below. "Not bad!" he called up to us. "It was fun!"

Aaron jumped next, followed by Eve, then me. Once we collected ourselves in the garage, we said our good-byes. I was left with the witch house to keep me company.

I went outside and watched my friends walk down the street. I turned around and walked in our front door. My mom was standing in the living room.

"Max, you startled me. I didn't hear you go out.

Come in here and sit with me for a few minutes." She patted the sofa cushion next to her and I sat down.

Mom began, "I know you were telling your friends all about your imaginary ghosts or whatever. Do you think that is good to do?"

"I don't know," I answered.

"My suggestion is that you keep your imaginary world to yourself. Is that all right with you?" She pushed for an answer.

"I'll try," I responded.

"That is all I can ask."

"Hey, Mom. We found this in one of those old trunks in the attic." I pulled the map out of my back pocket and handed it to her. "We thought it might be a treasure map."

Mom looked at the map. Then she looked at me and smiled. "Those trunks belonged to your grandmother. Your Aunt Elsie's been keeping them for me. I guess you were out walking Snowball when they arrived last Friday.

"I can't tell you what this map is for—it looks like directions to someone's house. But I can assure you it's not a map to hidden treasure."

Mom handed the map back to me. She continued to smile warmly. "Now, how about something to eat?"

"Thanks. I think I'll grab some fruit and go upstairs and read," I told her.

"That's fine. If you hear your brother while you're

up there, give me a call," she said as I headed for the kitchen.

"Sure, okay," I told her. I grabbed a banana and an apple and walked up the stairs.

Mom did not want me talking to my friends about what was going on, but I had to talk to somebody about it. Mom and Dad were just about ready to get my head examined. And I was starting to agree with them.

I pushed open the door to my bedroom. The curtain fluttered, and I realized I had forgotten to close my window like Mom had asked me to do. *I'll get to that before I go to sleep tonight,* I thought.

I sat at my desk, eating the fruit and reading one of my books. When I had finished eating, I changed into my pajamas then crawled under the bedcovers.

I read for about another hour before I turned off the light. After a day like I'd had I needed a good night's sleep.

I was awakened in the night by something crawling on top of me. I grunted loudly, "No." I stirred and felt something jump off the bed.

When I opened my eyes, all I saw was a shadow moving across the wall. The creature had run across the floor and vanished. I tried to yell, but my voice was caught in my throat.

The dark shadow was out to get me. Why? Why was the creature after me? I hadn't done anything except to move into the witch house.

It occurred to me that maybe the shadow I had seen had been Snowball. But Snowball would never run away from me like that.

I pulled back the covers and got out of bed. I tiptoed to the door of my bedroom. In a whisper, I called out into the hallway. "Snowball. Here, boy."

But Snowball was not there. He was probably asleep in Mom and Dad's room.

I went back to my bed. I lay there a long time listening in the dark. Then I pulled the covers up over my head and tried to will myself to sleep.

When the sun came up the next day, I quickly glanced around my room. Nothing looked out of the ordinary.

The thought came to me that I should look under my bed. If the creature had come back while I was sleeping, it could be hiding there.

I rolled on to my stomach and lay crosswise on the bed. I held onto the mattress and lowered my head toward the floor. I peered underneath the bed.

Just then something jumped me from behind.

24

I spun around quickly. Something was staring at me with black eyes. It had a black nose and white fur all over it. Snowball was just saying good morning.

"Don't do that, Snowball," I told him. "A guy could have a heart attack, even at my age."

He stuck out his tongue and barked. I knew he wanted to go outside.

I walked downstairs and let Snowball out the back door. I was thinking about last night's experience. The creature had been in my room. I wished someone had been there with me—a witness. If someone else had seen the creature then Mom and Dad would know that I wasn't just imagining it.

That gave me an idea.

I walked to the kitchen. Mom was feeding Tommy breakfast. She looked at me and smiled. "Did you sleep well last night, Max?"

"I think I fell asleep the minute my head hit the pillow," I answered. I was telling the truth. I had gone right to sleep. But of course I couldn't tell her that I was awakened in the middle of the night by some mysterious shadow creature.

"Hey, Mom. Would it be okay if I asked Jamal and Aaron to sleep over tonight?" That was my idea. I would have two witnesses if the creature came back.

Mom thought it was a great idea. She was happy that I was making friends so quickly in this town. "Why don't you call them after breakfast," Mom suggested.

I wolfed down a bowl of cereal, then went to the phone to call my new friends.

When I called Jamal, he started packing to come over before we got off the phone. Jamal had an adventurous spirit.

Aaron, however, was not so enthusiastic. He didn't like his last experience at my house. But he wanted to be part of the action.

I sat in the family room thinking of what we could do. I wanted other people to see and hear the things I had seen and heard.

I went upstairs to my room. I wanted to make up the bed and remove the empty packing boxes before my friends came over.

While I was making my bed a gentle breeze rustled the curtain, reminding me again that I had not closed my window.

I walked over to the window and tried to lower it. "This thing is really stuck," I said aloud. I thought I might be able to loosen it with a putty knife.

I knew we kept a putty knife in the toolbox. I had

not seen the toolbox since we moved, but I assumed Mom or Dad had put it in either the garage or the basement.

I walked downstairs and through the kitchen on my way to the garage. But when Mom saw me she decided to enlist me in some chores. The window would have to wait.

The chores took up the rest of the morning and most of the afternoon. Just as I finished everything Mom had asked me to do, the doorbell rang. It was Jamal and Aaron.

After tossing their sleeping bags and stuff in my bedroom we headed out to the woods to check on the tree house possibilities. There was that one tree we had investigated earlier that would be perfect. It had the type of branches that split from the trunk close to the bottom of the tree. The tree's arms spread wide and stretched into the sky.

Each of us climbed onto a branch of the tree. We stayed there a long time, planning how we could build our tree house. We decided we would start building it the following week.

After we had finalized our tree house plans we climbed down from the branches to head back toward the house. Jamal and Aaron had already started down the pathway while I was still climbing out of the tree. They were out of sight when I stepped onto the ground.

I started walking down the path. I still didn't see the

other two. I assumed that they were just far ahead of me.

After a couple of minutes I began to get nervous. Nothing looked familiar. This was only my second time to venture this far into the woods. I must have taken the wrong path.

I was standing beneath a large maple tree trying to get my bearings when I heard something that terrified me.

It was a bloodcurdling scream.

25

I nearly jumped a mile in the air. In fact, I jumped high enough to grab a branch that was hanging just above me. I was pulling myself up into the tree when I heard the scream again. It was closer this time. Too close as far as I was concerned.

Sitting on the tree branch, I looked over the woods to see who had screamed. No one was there.

Then another noise came from just below me. It was a horrible laugh. The kind of horrible laugh that says, "I got you again." It was Jamal.

"Where are you going, Max? Your house is back that way," Jamal said, pointing in the opposite direction from where I had been walking.

Aaron spoke up. "I think I just heard your Mom call us for dinner. Let's get back there before she thinks we all got lost for real."

We headed back to the house. This time I walked between the two of them to make sure that I didn't get lost.

After a dinner of my favorite, pizza with extra

cheese, we played video games and watched a movie till about ten o'clock. My mom had already gone to bed, but none of us were tired yet.

"Hey, I've got a great idea," Jamal said. He had one of those grins on his face—the kind he got when he had a plan. "The cemetery is only a couple of hundred yards on the other side of the woods. Now, I don't think that Max could lead us through it, but I'm pretty sure that I can pick out the pathway."

"What are you suggesting?" I asked, even though I knew what he had in mind.

"I'm saying that we ought to call Eve and then go see if the legend is true," Jamal answered.

"What legend?" I quizzed.

"Eve knows it best," Jamal answered. "Let's call her."

"It's too late to call," I told him.

"Yeah, you're right. We should probably just go by her house and throw stones at her window." Jamal didn't even wait for a response. He was walking toward the back door. Aaron and I followed him outside.

Eve lived only a few houses down from me. When we got there I was surprised at how easy it was to get her attention. She was sitting next to an open window watching TV. Jamal told her the idea and asked her to tell me the legend of the cemetery.

In a few minutes she was out of the house and we were sitting around her picnic table in the backyard. The woods bordering the yard looked dark and foreboding. The light of the full moon cast long shadows across the yard. The tree limbs above the table drew black, wild lines on our faces. To sum it up, it was creepy looking.

Eve began the tale. "This was something my older brother told me. He heard it from another kid in the senior high youth group. And he heard it from a kid whose sister actually saw it.

"It happened about ten years ago. Some kids from the high school were having a party. A few of the kids suggested that everyone go to the cemetery to tell ghost stories. What the others didn't know was that this group of kids had gotten together earlier and planned to scare their friends once they got inside the cemetery.

"Two guys agreed to go ahead of the group and set up some things that would look like ghosts. One of the town's ghost stories is about a train engineer who was run over by a train, and now he walks the tracks next to the cemetery each night. According to the story, the ghost carries a lantern and people can see it swinging on the tracks.

"So the kids went there at midnight."

I interrupted her. "Eve, then there aren't really any ghosts. It's nothing but a story made up by high school kids?"

"No, let me finish. The two boys went ahead of the rest of the group and set up a lantern that swung from a tree. They attached a fishing line to it, and then ran the line a few hundred feet away.

"When the others showed up, the two boys joined them. They were joking around and suddenly a lantern came down the track and toward them. It was swinging from side to side just like in the legend."

"I still don't see the point in the story," I broke in.

Jamal was getting frustrated with me. "If you let her finish the story, you'll find something out about your new house."

I nodded okay.

Eve continued. "Everyone who wasn't in on the joke got really scared, but the ones who were playing the joke on the others acted extremely brave. Except for the two who had set up the lantern.

"The lantern started swinging, but it was coming from the other end of the tracks. It was the real thing because the one the boys had rigged would have come from the other direction.

"When the two said it was for real, everyone started running. But they didn't get very far." Eve's eyes opened wide as if she were frightened. "As they moved through these woods, a real ghost came swooping down out of the trees and nearly grabbed one of them."

My curiosity was piqued. "Where does my house fit in?" I asked.

"That comes a little later," Eve answered. "The group ran through the woods as fast as they could, but

85

when they got to the edge of the woods by your house, there stood the witch. She had a broom in her hand and was waiting for them."

"What did she do? Did she put a spell on them? Did she turn one of them into a cat or something?" I asked.

"No. They turned around and ran back into the woods, but the witch followed them. When the kids finally came out of the woods three days later, their hair was white as snow. Eventually, each one ended up in a mental hospital."

"That is, except for one," Aaron said.

"What do you mean by 'except for one'?" I asked. I was sure that the fright was starting to show on my face. "Who was the one, and what happened to him?"

"One of the two that planted the fake lantern roams the woods every night. His ghost is trying to make up for the wrong he did. He walks through the graves and he floats through the woods seeking those who violate his cemetery," Eve said. "He yells—"

Behind me a voice yelled, *"Beware!"*

It wasn't Eve.

26

"Ah!" I shrieked and fell off my seat.

As I lay on my back looking up, I saw the face of Jamal howling above me. He had done it again.

I extended my hand toward him. "Jamal, the least you could do is help me up."

He grabbed my hand. Instead of him pulling me up, I shifted my weight and pulled him down.

"We're even now," I told him.

"Don't worry, I'll get you again," he shot back at me.

I was sure that Jamal was already planning the next big joke, and I would not know when and where it was coming from. I looked at Eve and asked, "So, how much of the story was true and how much was made up so that Jamal could scare me?"

"The whole thing is true as far as I know. I told it to you the way it was told to me. I'm sure my brother told it to me the way he heard it. Even the part about 'Beware' is true," she told me.

"Are we ready?" Jamal asked.

"For what? First you tell me this story about ghosts

in the cemetery and in the woods. Then you ask me to go out there and face them. I don't think I'm ready to do that," I said strongly.

"All right, then we go in without you," Jamal said.

Aaron moved closer to me and said, "I'm scared, too, but I've decided that someone has to find out if this legend is true. It might as well be us."

I thought for a few moments and spoke. "I guess any guy who is living with a monster in his house should be brave enough to face a couple of ghosts."

Everyone exchanged high fives. Then we moved carefully through the night across Eve's backyard.

With only the moonlight to guide us, we moved into the woods. In the woods, the moonlight was barely visible. I wasn't sure that I really wanted to do this, but I didn't want my friends to think I was chicken.

"Does anyone know where we are going?" Aaron asked.

"Great time to ask that, Aaron," I told him.

Eve spoke up. "I do. I've done this before. Just follow the well-worn path. People said that the witch used to walk this pathway nightly to find her victims."

"Or to bury them," Jamal added in a spooky voice.

I kept looking down at my feet to make sure that I didn't trip on anything. I tried to memorize each stone's position. I had a feeling that we might have to be running out of there very quickly, and I didn't want to fall with a ghost coming after me.

We moved silently. Then Eve stopped.

"What was that?" she said.
"What?" I asked. I was really spooked now.
"Shh!" Eve put her index finger to her lips.
I listened. Then I heard it. We all heard it.
There were voices.

27

None of us moved. I felt like I was an ice sculpture. I was stiff. I felt cold, but I was sweating.

Eve motioned for us to hide. We did so. Then she crept slowly toward the voices. She was keeping low as she edged through the shadows. I watched her kneel behind a large bush. Eve saw something.

She turned around and motioned for Jamal, Aaron, and me to join her. When I got to the bush, I knelt behind it and peered through the leaves. I couldn't believe what I saw.

A group of older kids were standing in a circle. I could not figure out what was going on. A tall guy was talking to the group. I assumed he was the leader.

I overheard him say, "If anybody is scared then they can leave now."

The other kids made no response. I thought they were more afraid of the tall guy than they were of the graveyard.

Aaron whispered to me, "What do you think they're doing out here?"

"The same thing we're doing," I whispered. "I'll bet they want to see if the legend is true." I was going to say more, but the tall guy started speaking again.

"The rules are that whoever stays in the cemetery the longest is the winner, and the first one out buys everyone else breakfast," he said.

I looked at Aaron. He was wrinkling his nose and tilting his head. He let out a thunderous sneeze.

The gang of older kids looked our way.

"Run for it!" Jamal yelled. We did.

I could hear the sound of feet pounding on hard dirt behind me. Two of the older kids were pursuing me. I tried to lose them but ended up running right through the middle of the graves. I was scared enough with two guys chasing me. I didn't need to be grabbed by some ghost, goblin, or ghoul.

I saw what I thought was an opening to the woods. I made a sharp turn and I tripped and fell flat on my face. Four hands grabbed me by my shirt and belt. They yanked me to my feet.

"Why were you spying on us?" a sweaty boy screamed into my face.

"We weren't. We came out to see if the legend is true," I said as my knees grew weak. My legs were ready to buckle.

"Maybe we can use him as bait for the ghost of the lantern. What do you think?" the sweaty one asked his friend.

He never had a chance to answer. Both boys saw

the expression of terror on my face. Speechless, I raised my hand and pointed. They turned to see what I was pointing at.

A shiny, fluorescent white form was slowly floating down from the trees above us. There was no doubt about it. It was a ghost.

28

As the ghost neared us, the two attackers took off running. I wanted to run, too, but my feet wouldn't move. I was paralyzed by fear.

The ghost continued to float toward me. Now my knees buckled and I fell to the ground. I hid my face in my hands. I wasn't sure why I did that. Maybe I thought the ghost would not see me hiding under my hands.

I waited. Nothing grabbed me. I looked up for my unwanted visitor. But now the ghost was floating higher into the air and away from me. The ghost had saved me from my attackers.

I stood up and brushed the dirt from my clothes. I looked around and realized that I was lost. I wasn't sure which direction led to my house.

I moved through the graves, trying to remember where I had been before. But I had been running too fast to notice things. Nothing looked familiar. I was feeling scared and frustrated. Why had I listened to my new friends? They had gotten me into something that I did not want to be involved in.

I walked through the cemetery slowly. I saw the clearing where the older kids had been. As I headed toward it I thought about the ghost. *Was it for real? Are there such things?* My parents had told me there was no such thing as ghosts, and yet I saw one. My mind got cloudier than before. Nothing made sense.

I got to the clearing. From there I saw the bush we had been hiding behind. I had some hope. I now knew the direction that I needed to go, but I was not sure I knew the pathway. It didn't matter, I had to make a decision.

I approached the bush slowly and quietly. I didn't know why I was being so quiet. My friends had run away. The older kids had run away. Even the ghost had left me.

I was feeling very alone. I gave a heavy and loud sigh and then I heard a popping sound behind me.

I turned around and saw a puff of smoke rising from the ground. Then a booming voice echoed through the woods.

It said one word: "Beware!"

29

This time the fear didn't paralyze me. It sent a rush of adrenaline through my body and I sprinted through the graves like I had the football and was running for the winning touchdown.

But all my running managed to do was get me lost again.

I skidded to a stop. I saw a large mausoleum where they did aboveground burials. I walked toward it, thinking that if I climbed on top of it I could get a better look at the area. Maybe I could see my house through the trees.

I was willing to try anything. The legend was true, and the ghost was after me. I had to get out of that cemetery as quickly as I could.

Once on top of the mausoleum, I looked all around me. I had been heading in the right direction before the "Beware!" warning. I would have to go back that way.

I slid down a statue of an angel next to the burial building. I ran toward the clearing and then the bush.

I had made it past the spot where the voice in the midst of the smoke had yelled "Beware!" With only a few more steps I would be beyond the graveyard.

But like everything else that happened that night, my plan did not work out as I had hoped. As I reached the last grave another puff of smoke rose from the ground and into the air. It looked like a ghost rising from the grave. Then I heard the warning again: "Beware!"

I agreed. I wanted to beware, and I thought the best way to do it was to get out of the cemetery as fast as I could. Again, I plunged into the woods.

By now my legs were aching. I didn't know how I could keep running. Once I was in the safety of the trees, I slowed to a walk.

The moonlight fell through the trees, giving me enough light to see a path. Then I heard a twig crackle in the trees beside me.

I turned to my left to see what had made the sound. Something grabbed my right arm.

I screamed, "No, get away from me!" I spun around. My whole body went limp. What I saw surprised me.

Aaron had grabbed me. "Max, we were really worried about you," he said with real concern in his voice. Eve and Jamal were standing behind him.

"We were on our way back to find you. As soon as we hit the grass in your backyard, we realized that you were not with us. I got scared that the other guys may have grabbed you. I can't tell you how glad I am to see you right now," Eve told me.

"So?" Jamal said, raising his eyebrows.

"So, what?" I asked him back.

"So what happened?"

"If I told you, you would not believe me."

Eve looked at me and said, "Try us."

I started telling them the story, but when I got to the part about the ghost saving me from the two guys who had jumped me, Jamal stopped me.

"Are you trying to say that a ghost floated down out of the trees and saved you from those guys? Wow! We've got to go back and see this," he said.

"No way!" I said firmly. "Besides, that's not all that happened. The ghost that cries 'Beware!' jumped out twice. It was really frightening. The voice was big. It sounded like it was resonating off the walls of the Grand Canyon. That spooked me big time."

"I've got to see all this," Jamal insisted.

Eve said, "Me, too."

She grabbed Aaron and me by the hands and started dragging us along the pathway back to the graveyard. I didn't want to go back there. But I didn't want to get lost in the woods by myself either.

In a few minutes, we stepped out of the woods and into the cemetery. I pointed to the last spot where I had seen a puff of smoke. Jamal and Eve moved to that spot. They stood next to the tombstone and began to search for something. They did not know what, and neither did I.

"There's nothing here. I don't think you saw anything. I think the fright of being caught by those other kids caused you to see things," Jamal told me.

I was almost ready to agree with him when it happened again. A puff of smoke rose next to him. Then the voice came thundering from above us: "Beware!"

30

"What was that?" Aaron said as he grabbed my arm. Jamal and Eve leaped away from the tombstone.

"That was one of the ghosts," I answered.

Eve turned to Jamal. "Jamal, I've changed my mind about seeing the ghosts. Let's get out of here."

I agreed quickly and so did Aaron, but Jamal was a little harder to convince. He said to us, "I just want to see where the ghost floated in the air."

"Then can we leave after that?" I asked.

"Take him to the floating ghost," Aaron said.

I began leading them through the woods to the spot where I thought that I had seen the floating ghost. I actually wanted it to appear again. The sooner we saw the floating phantom, the quicker we could get Jamal out of here.

I took a few wrong turns. That could be expected since most of the graves looked alike. Then I saw a tombstone with a name on it that I remembered.

I took another few steps and then stopped. I heard a voice. It was a soft voice, and I could not make out what it was saying. I stopped the others by raising my hand in the air. We moved into the shadows of a small grove of trees.

Eve whispered softly, "Max, what is it?"

"I hear the voice of a man right where the floating ghost appeared. Either it is the ghost talking to itself, or it has a captive," I said with as faint a voice as possible. "I'm going to find out what it is. Wait here with the others."

"No, I think we all need to stay together. If you go then we go with you," she insisted.

"Tell Aaron and Jamal what we're doing. I'm going to creep ahead a few more feet and wait for you," I said as I slipped deeper into the small grove. I should not have done that. I got closer than I expected. In fact, I was so close that I could see a tall, thin creature bending over something. About the same time I saw the creature, I attracted its attention.

My eyes met the eyes of the creature. I still could not see exactly what it was. I did not hang around to find out either. I spun on my heels and tore out of there. That was my second mistake. As I turned and ran I plowed into my three friends. The four of us went sprawling onto the ground.

I tried to scramble to my feet but I kept slipping. My blunder was going to cost us. I heard the thud of feet trampling over dried grass, sticks, and leaves.

This would be the second time I was caught by something in this same spot.

A hand reached down and grabbed me by the belt, yanking me to my feet. I twisted around, expecting to see the ghost.

31

"The cemetery is closed after dark, kids. You'll have to go home now."

"What? Who are you?" I stammered out. It wasn't a ghost after all. It was a man.

"I should be the one asking the questions, but I can see that I have scared the four of you quite enough. My name is Ezekiel Jones. I'm the caretaker here in Oakwood Hills Cemetery. Our slogan is: People are dying to get in." He started laughing, then noticed we weren't. "That's a little cemetery caretaker joke. I guess you didn't get it."

Mr. Jones helped us up. "I hope you're not part of the group of vandals who were in the graveyard a little earlier."

"No, sir. We saw them, though," Jamal said.

"Their antics set off several of my little creations. If I didn't know what they were, I would be afraid and run like a bunch of scared, clucking chickens out of here," the old man said.

"Creations? What do you mean by creations?" Aaron chimed in.

The caretaker motioned for us to sit down. We sat together on the ground. He looked at us and smiled. Mr. Jones picked up a piece of white cloth lying on the dirt. Holding the cloth in his hands, he began to explain.

"Several years ago, youngsters from the local high school started coming to the cemetery. They were up to no good. I was getting too old to chase them around, so I put together these fright sights."

"Fright sights? Do you mean like the puffs of smoke and the voice that said 'Beware!'?" I asked.

"Yes, I have several of those. If you step on one of the trigger points a puff of smoke is released from a spray can under the ground. It blows into the air. The voice is a tape recording that comes on whenever the smoke triggers are tripped.

"And this guy," he held up the white cloth, "is Old Goober the Ghost. He is nothing but cheesecloth and one of those glow sticks. When its switch is tripped, Goober slides down this wire and up the other one. The glow stick is what really makes it frightening.

"This has been working for years. And since you know the truth, then you are sworn to secrecy. Okay?" he asked with a wink.

We all agreed in unison.

"So there aren't really any ghosts in here?" Eve asked.

"Absolutely not," Mr. Jones responded. "After living next door to this graveyard for over forty years, I can assure you that no ghost walks through this quiet little resting spot for the dearly departed.

"Now, let me give you four one of my flashlights so you can find your way home safely. You can just drop it off tomorrow sometime." He turned to dig through a bag he carried with him.

"Mr. Jones, what about the lantern that swings on the tracks?" Eve asked.

He laughed. "It's my wife and me signaling one another. If it is swinging then I need to come home. Now, get on out of here and don't let any more ghosts get you."

With the flashlight, we were able to make it through the cemetery and the woods quickly. The whole time we talked about Mr. Jones and how neat his little fright sights were. Jamal wanted to bring some of the other kids from the youth group out the next night.

Aaron protested. "Jamal, we can't do that. Mr. Jones told us a secret that we need to keep. None of the other kids should know about this."

All of us were fairly quiet as we walked Eve back to her house.

When we got there she said goodnight and walked to the front door. She turned back toward us before going in the house. She smiled and said, "That was great fun. It sure made a boring evening a lot more interesting. See you all tomorrow morning."

When we got to my house we slipped in the back

door. I was about four steps into the house when something jumped in front of me.

one. I was look-ing, stepping in the dose-what
seeming noised in front.

"Max, where have you been?" My mom had fury in her eyes.

I couldn't lie. "We all went to the cemetery where we saw a ghost float through the air and puffs of smoke that came out of the ground and we heard a voice that said 'Beware.'" I was explaining so fast my words seemed to run together.

"I guess we will have to talk about this tomorrow morning when you are ready to tell what really happened," she said. "Now, all of you, go to bed!"

We headed upstairs to my room.

When we got there Aaron and Jamal rolled out their sleeping bags on the floor. After we changed into our pajamas, Aaron and Jamal got into their sleeping bags. I turned off the light and crawled underneath the bedcovers.

As we lay there in the dark I began to tell them about being awakened the previous night by something crawling on my bed.

"Did you get a look at it?" Jamal asked.

"No. When I stirred, it jumped off the bed. But I saw its shadow on the wall," I explained.

"What do you think it was?" Aaron asked. He sounded nervous.

"I don't know," I said. "But the shadow was pretty big."

"Max, turn the light on," Aaron said. "This conversation is getting me spooked."

I reached over and turned on the bedside lamp.

"Thanks," Aaron said.

"Your folks haven't seen anything, right?" Jamal asked.

"No. They would have told me if they had seen something," I answered.

Jamal furrowed his brow. He seemed to be thinking deeply about something. After a few seconds he asked, "Max, why do you think it came into *your* room last night?"

"Well . . ." I didn't know the answer to that question. After a few moments I shrugged my shoulders to indicate that I didn't know why.

"I think it came after you because you got to close to a secret," Jamal said.

"What secret?" Aaron asked before I got a chance.

"Remember when we were in the cellar looking at the hole Snowball had dug? Aaron, you said that maybe the witch had buried human bones in that cellar. I made a joke of it to scare all of you . . ." Jamal paused. "But maybe you were right."

"So you believe that the witch really did bury bones of her victims in the cellar? And somehow she knows that we have uncovered her secret burial place?" Aaron said.

"Exactly. And that's why the creature came after Max last night. Max was the only one in the house last night who was there when Snowball uncovered the secret," Jamal said.

"Wait a minute," I said. "We didn't find any bones. So Snowball really didn't uncover anything."

"But if that creature was hiding somewhere in the basement when we were in the cellar, it could have overheard our conversation," Jamal said. "It could have reported to the witch what we had talked about."

"I get it," Aaron said. "And if she thought we even suspected what she had done . . ." He stopped talking. He had a worried look on his face.

"What's wrong, Aaron? What are you thinking?" I asked.

"If the witch knows that Jamal and I are spending the night here, then she's sure to send that creature back to get all of us," he said, shuddering.

I shuddered, too. If Aaron and Jamal were right, then the three of us were in big trouble. Only Eve was safe, but for how long? Would the creature go after her?

I was about to tell Aaron and Jamal that we would definitely leave the light on all night. But the sound I heard scared me so badly that I couldn't speak.

It was the moaning sound.

Aaron and Jamal sprang from their sleeping bags.

Aaron looked white as a ghost. "What's making that noise?" he asked.

"It's the creature," I said. "It's in the room next door."

The next few moments seemed like hours. The three of us sat on my bed, listening to the horrible moan.

Finally, Jamal spoke. "We can't just sit here and wait for whatever that thing is to come and get us. We've got to make the first move."

"What do you think we should do?" I asked in a shaky voice.

"We've got to go in that room," he answered.

"Aaron, I'm scared, too," I said. "But Jamal's right. We can't just lie here and wait for the creature to attack us. We've got to go after it first."

Aaron didn't say anything right away. He looked down at the floor. After a few seconds passed he said, "Okay. I'm with you. Let's go."

We got up and walked out my bedroom door.

I stood at the door to the spare room listening to the moaning. My mouth was dry with fear. I turned around and saw my two friends. Jamal had my baseball bat in his hand. Aaron had my baseball glove. Why the glove? I didn't know. I guess he thought he was going to catch the creature with it.

I opened the door slowly. The moaning stopped. Jamal reached around me and pushed on the door hard. It went flying open. My eyes raced around the room. I took a step inside. Jamal raised the bat and Aaron extended his gloved hand.

Just then something black flew out the window. We were too late to catch it. Even with the baseball glove.

Frustrated and scared, we went back to my room. Jamal thought the creature looked to be about four feet tall. Aaron thought it was more like three feet tall. I wasn't sure. It just scared me.

"Listen, we've got to warn Eve," I said. "She knows the witch's secret, too."

"We can't tell her now," Aaron said. "It's too late. We'll wake her parents."

"They're sure to answer the phone, and what are we going to say?" Jamal said. "If we tell them their daughter's life is threatened by a monster, they'll think we're pulling a prank . . . or that we're crazy."

Just then we heard the squeak of a hinge. We spun around and looked at the bedroom door.

Something was pushing it open.

Mom poked her head inside the room. "I can't believe you boys are still awake." She yawned. "Don't you know what time it is?"

"Sorry, Mom. We didn't mean to wake you up."

"It's okay. But turn out the light now and get some sleep."

Mom shut the door behind her.

Aaron and Jamal climbed back into their sleeping bags. I switched off the lamp and crawled beneath the covers.

"I don't think I can sleep," Aaron whispered.

"Me either," I whispered back. "But let's lie quietly. Keep your ears open for any strange noise."

I closed my eyes and said a silent prayer that we would be safe for the night.

When I opened my eyes the room was lit with sunlight. I had fallen asleep after all. I turned over and looked off the edge of my bed. My two friends were sleeping.

As quietly as possible, I got out of bed and walked toward the bedroom door. Carefully, I stepped over Jamal.

Something grabbed my ankle. I flinched and tried to break loose. I looked down at my leg.

Jamal was holding my ankle.

He looked up at me. "Got you," he said.

I sighed in relief. I grinned at him and asked, "Are we even now?"

Jamal laughed. "Yeah," he said. "We're even."

Aaron began to stir in his sleeping bag. He sat up and rubbed his eyes. "What time is it?" he asked.

"A little after eight," I replied. "Anybody hungry?"

"I'm starved," Jamal said.

"Get dressed and come down to the kitchen. I'll fix us something to eat," I said.

After breakfast I called Eve. I told her about the creature and how we all were in danger.

"So you guys really saw it?" she asked.

"We got a glimpse of it as it jumped out the window," I explained. "Can you come over here? I think the four of us need to come up with a plan."

"I'm on my way," she said before she hung up the phone.

When Eve arrived, Jamal, Aaron, and I reported on last night's adventure.

"Last night was the second time I heard the creature moan," I told her.

"I don't think I'll ever forget that sound," Aaron added.

"Me either," said Jamal. "It was the creepiest sound I've ever heard. But I wouldn't exactly call it a moan. It was more high-pitched than a moan."

"That's true," Aaron said. "I don't know how to describe it. You'd just have to hear it."

We were sitting around the kitchen table. I heard Mom's footsteps coming toward us. I motioned for everyone to be quiet.

"Hi, Eve," Mom said. She was holding Tommy in the crook of her right arm. "Good to see you again."

"Hi, Mrs. Walker," Eve replied with a smile.

"Max, I've got to go out for a while. I'm out of printer cartridges. You four hold down the fort while I'm gone, okay?"

"Sure thing, Mom," I replied.

I was relieved that Mom didn't say anything about our escapade last night. I knew she trusted me not to get into any trouble. But I was feeling a little guilty about leaving the house so late last night and worrying her like I did. I knew she would talk to me about it later when my friends left.

"I think we need to comb the whole house," Eve said, picking the discussion back up. "The creature must be hiding in here somewhere."

"That's a good idea, Eve," I said.

"Let's devise a plan," Jamal said. "First, we each need to carry something for protection. Max, what have you got besides a baseball bat?"

"Well, Mom and Dad have some golf clubs."

"Great," Jamal said. "Three of us will each carry a golf club."

"I think we should start looking in the basement," I said.

"First I'd like to see where you saw it last night," Eve requested.

"Okay. We show Eve where we saw the creature last night, then we go to the basement," Jamal said. "If we don't find it there, we proceed to the first floor, then the second floor, and finally the attic."

"Let's get going," Eve said.

Just then we heard a scratching noise. It was coming from the back of the house.

"Wait here," I instructed the others.

I crept toward the sliding glass doors that opened onto the deck. The scratching sound grew louder.

I walked closer to the glass doors and crouched behind a chair. I peered over the back of the chair and looked out the glass door.

Snowball was scratching frantically against the glass door. He wanted to come inside the house.

I released a long exhale and let him in. "Come on, Buddy. We've got a creature to catch."

He followed me back to the kitchen where I had left my friends.

114

"You can relax for now. It was only Snowball," I said. Aaron reached down and scratched Snowball under his chin.

I went to the garage and got three golf clubs. Then the four of us went upstairs. Snowball followed us.

"We've got to get the baseball bat out of my room first," I said.

We went to my room, and I retrieved the bat from where Jamal had put it the night before. We turned around to go back into the hallway.

That's when the moaning began.

35

I jumped about a foot in the air. I looked at the others. Aaron had turned pale, and Eve's eyes were as big as saucers. Jamal had his eyes closed. I think he was praying.

"Is that the . . . sound you heard last night?" Eve sputtered.

"Yes," I answered in a whisper. I hadn't meant to talk so softly, but I was scared.

By this time we couldn't tell where the sound was coming from.

Aaron inched over to the floor register. "I think the sound is coming up through here," he said.

"That's the heat register," I said. "The creature must be in the basement near the furnace."

"Then we better get down there now," Jamal said.

"I'm not so sure about this anymore, Max." Aaron was shaking. "Talking about finding the creature is one thing. I don't think I'm ready to come face-to-face with it."

"We don't have a choice, Aaron. Either we find it, or it comes after us," I said.

Aaron didn't say anything in response. He nodded his head to indicate he understood.

We slipped into the hallway and raced downstairs to the basement steps.

At the top of the steps I stopped and turned around to face the others. "Everyone armed and ready?"

My friends brandished their golf clubs. I still had the baseball bat. "Here we go."

I almost tripped over Snowball, who sped down the steps ahead of us.

I had just stepped onto the basement floor when, all of a sudden, Snowball started barking. Then we heard a noise. It sounded like boxes being overturned.

Aaron screamed. Jamal and Eve clung to the back of my shirt.

I was shaking. I wanted to turn and race back up the steps. But I couldn't leave Snowball down here unprotected.

I took a step forward. I raised the bat in case something jumped out at me from around the corner.

"Let's get out of here," Aaron whispered.

"I've got to rescue my dog," I said. Snowball was still barking loudly.

"We've got to stick together, Aaron," Eve said. "Stay close to me."

Together we inched our way around the corner.

Nothing jumped out at us. I reached up and pulled the string to turn on the overhead light.

Snowball was standing near one of the wall shelves barking wildly. Two empty boxes lay on the floor. *Something must have knocked them off the shelf,* I thought.

"Come, Buddy," I commanded. Snowball ignored my command. He continued to bark at the shelf.

From where I stood I couldn't see what Snowball was barking at. I summoned all my courage and carefully stepped over to him.

I looked up at the shelf. All I could see were more boxes. Was something hiding up there?

I knelt down and patted Snowball. "What is it, boy? What's in here?" I wished that Snowball could talk so he could tell me what he had seen.

I looked up at my friends. Jamal was inching his way toward the cellar. He had the golf club raised.

The cellar door was open. Had we left it open the last time we were down here? Or had someone, or something, else opened the door?

Jamal peered through the cellar doorway, then turned back toward me. "Max, is there a flashlight down here?" he called.

"I think there's one upstairs in the cabinet under the kitchen sink," I said. "I'll get it."

"No, I'll go," Aaron said. Before I could argue he turned and sped toward the stairway. I heard his footsteps racing up the stairs. For a moment I wondered if he would come back. I knew he was scared. But a few seconds later I heard him racing back down the steps.

"Here," he said, handing the flashlight to Jamal.

Jamal flipped on the flashlight and entered the cellar doorway. All of a sudden Snowball stopped barking and raced to follow Jamal.

I watched Snowball run into the cellar, then I turned to look back up at the shelf. Whatever had knocked those boxes off was gone now. Or was hiding somewhere else in the basement.

"Come here!" Jamal shouted.

Eve, Aaron, and I ran to the cellar. Inside, Snowball was sniffing near the hole he had dug. Now he began to dig some more.

Jamal shined the light on the hole just as Snowball clamped down on something with his jaws. He held the object between his teeth and backed away from the hole.

"What's he got?" Aaron asked.

Jamal shined the beam on Snowball's muzzle.

The object was slender and the color of flesh.

Eve gasped. "It looks like a human finger!" she said.

36

Jamal was shaking so much that he couldn't hold the flashlight steady. It slipped from his hand and hit the dirt floor next to where Snowball stood.

Snowball bolted out the cellar door, the object still clinched between his teeth.

Eve bent down and picked up the flashlight. I ran out of the cellar in pursuit of Snowball. "Snowball, no!" I shouted in my most commanding voice.

Snowball stopped and dropped the object on the floor. He cowered as I stepped closer to him.

My stomach was churning with fear as I glimpsed the object that lay on the floor before me. I knelt down near the object and rolled it closer to me with the baseball bat.

Underneath the overhead light of the basement, I got a good look at it. I reached down with my free hand and picked it up. I couldn't help it. I started to laugh.

By now my three friends were standing behind me. "How can you laugh at that?" Eve said.

"Look at it and you'll see," I told her. I turned around and held it toward her face. She jumped back.

"It's pizza crust," I said between giggles. "I don't like to eat the edges of the crust, but Snowball does. We've been eating a lot of pizza lately. I bet he has a dozen of these crust edges buried in there."

Aaron and Jamal started to laugh, and soon Eve broke out in laughter, too.

But our laughter was interrupted by a loud crash in the far corner of the basement.

Snowball began barking again and ran to where the crash had come from. Again I raised my bat. I eased over to where Snowball was barking. A glass jar lay broken on the floor.

I looked up at the shelf on the wall. I screamed.

On the shelf was a large black creature. It glared at me with big yellow eyes.

Eve rushed to my side. She looked up and gasped. "That's the biggest cat I've ever seen," she exclaimed.

The cat let out a tremendous yowl.

Jamal and Aaron ran over to us. "That's the noise. The creature's . . ." Jamal broke off. He looked up to where Eve and I were staring. He jumped back. Then he looked at the shelf again. "Man, that's one big black cat," he said.

"So that's what we heard and saw?" a voice said. It was Aaron.

The cat let out another shrill yowl.

"Yeah. That's it," I said.

"Here kitty, kitty." Jamal tried to coax the cat down. But Snowball was still barking, and the cat stayed on the shelf.

"How did it get in here?" Eve asked.

"I think I know," I said. "The windows in my room and the sewing room are open. They're stuck. I was supposed to close them but I forgot about it.

"Anyway, there's that big tree outside those windows. The cat must have climbed up the tree and jumped in through the window."

"Okay. That explains how it got in the rooms upstairs. But how did it get in the basement?" Aaron asked. "You keep the door to the basement stairs closed, right?"

Aaron had a point. Except for when we were moving boxes and that night I had encountered the creature— the cat—downstairs, the door had been closed.

"I think I know the answer to that," Jamal said. "Follow me."

Jamal led us back to the coal cellar.

"Eve, hand me the flashlight," he said.

Eve gave the flashlight to Jamal and he pointed the beam to a large hole in the foundation near the coal chute.

"When I was in here earlier looking around with the flashlight I saw that gaping hole," Jamal said. "I didn't think much about it then."

"Dad said he heard that the woman who lived here

before us had a lot of cats," I said. "Maybe she adopted a lot of stray cats—"

"And this one got left behind," Eve completed my thought.

"Poor kitty," Jamal said. "Maybe we can coax him down with some food."

I picked up the barking Snowball, and we went upstairs to look in the cupboards. I thought we probably had a can of tuna. Just then Mom walked in.

"Anybody hungry? We could order pizza."

I started laughing.

"What's so funny?" Mom gave me a quizzical look.

"It's a long story, Mom," I said between laughs.

I had a feeling it would be a long time before I wanted to eat pizza with extra cheese again.

Screams came from everywhere. High-pitched screeches filled the air behind me, and earsplitting bellows rushed at me. I stood with my eyes wide and staring. Kids raced by me.

Standing on the front sidewalk of my new middle school, I stared at the old red brick walls. A mixture of feelings ran through me as fast as the kids who ripped by.

I was still frozen in place when it sounded again. The final bell signaled the beginning of my first day at Crider Middle School.

We had moved from a big city to a small town in the midwest because Dad thought that raising a family in a small town would be ideal.

But now I was alone.

I was lost.

And I was a little frightened.

But I had to go in.

The stone steps leading up to the old-fashioned

wooden doors were worn from all the years and all the kids. I went as slowly as I could.

The halls were empty by the time I reached the entrance, and it was spooky. As I stepped inside, the high ceilings, old lockers, and linoleum floor worked together to make each step echo as if I was in a huge cave. I knew anyone listening would be thinking, She must be that new girl.

"That new girl" was exactly who I was. I didn't know anyone. I didn't like the idea of being looked at by everyone who already knew everyone else.

On top of being new, I was tall for my age. My height came in handy for the basketball team, but it made me stand out above the crowd. Literally. Especially when I was trying to melt into the wall.

I stopped in front of the school's office and sucked in a breath. As I reached for the doorknob, the door flew open in front of me, but I didn't see anyone on the other side. What happened?

Cautiously, I stepped through the doorway and into the office. With a small, quiet shuffle I made my way toward the office counter.

Several women and men moved in a flurry of activity from one desk to another. No one noticed me. That was good. Not every person in the school would be staring at me.

Suddenly the door crashed shut behind me. I turned to face a tall, thick man with hair that stuck straight up in the air. His nose was large and hooked. His arms were so long that they nearly reached his knees.

If he hadn't been between me and the door, I would have been out of there and home in three seconds.

He reached a long, bony-fingered hand toward me and said to the milling faculty, "Ladies and gentlemen of the Crider Middle School staff, I would like you to meet our newest student, Caitlin James."

Every eye and head was fixed on me. I felt like a fish in the first-grade aquarium with the whole room's eyes so close that I could see myself in every one of them.

"Welcome, Caitlin," the staff said in unison as their faces lit up with smiles.

I tried to say "Hi," but my mouth was so dry that only the *i* came out in a high-pitched whistle. My face turned red. All I wanted to do was race out of there and not come back. But the tall man was between me and the door. So I cleared my throat and tried it again: "Hello." It came out fine that time, and I relaxed.

"We have been expecting you. We all know how difficult it is at a new school on the first day, so we wanted to make it easy for you. Come into my office and I'll tell you about your day."

I followed him into his office—the principal's office. That was my first clue that he must be Dr. Wiser. He spent the next few minutes shoving papers in my hands and explaining my schedule to me.

When he finished, I asked about the topic dear to

my heart. "Dr. Wiser, can I still try out for the basketball team?"

"Caitlin, the coach is expecting you after school. I hope you brought your practice clothes."

"Right in my bag," I said as I lifted my gym bag off the floor.

"I think that we already wrote and told you that since we are a small school we don't have separate girls' and boys' basketball teams. Three other girls are on the team. From what I hear about your ability, you may end up being our star player," the principal informed me.

In the last school, I was the leading scorer in our division. Being tall for my age was great on the basketball court. The court was where I did my best work, but this would be my first official coed team.

Dr. Wiser's voice snapped me back from my school daze. "Caitlin, let me show you to your locker." We got up and headed out the door and down the cavernous hallway as he talked softly in a voice most people reserve for the library.

"Since the school is so old, we barely have enough lockers for students. In the past, some kids have even shared lockers. The good news is that there is one locker left. The bad news is that it is in the farthest, most out-of-the-way place."

We walked around several corners and eventually got to a short corridor. I headed back toward the end with Dr. Wiser. The farther in we got, the worse it smelled.

I kept gagging with each step until we could go no farther.

Two lockers stood next to each other at the end of the hall. No wonder my locker was still empty. The one next to it smelled like rotten eggs mixed with old, sweaty gym clothes. Green goo oozed from its vents.

"Dr. Wiser, what's that smell?"

"You'll get used to it. We all do. Your locker is the one on the right. This one next to yours," he said as his hand went near the left one but did not touch it, "is not currently habitable."

"You can say that again," I told him as I tossed my bag into my locker and backed out of the small corridor as fast as I could.

Dr. Wiser spent the rest of the morning showing me around the school. By the time we finished, I actually knew where everything was and some of the shortcuts through the halls.

At lunchtime he dropped me off at the cafeteria and pointed out a table of kids. He told me that they were waiting to meet me after I bought my lunch. The cafeteria food smelled good compared to the stinky locker that had so recently attacked my nose.

I was grateful to see some faces that smiled at me as I guided my tray with mystery meat, shriveled green beans, and a hard-as-rock peanut butter cookie back to their table.

"Hi, I'm Scott. Dr. Wiser said that you would be arriving here today. We're really glad to have you at Crider Middle School. How's your first day going?"

All those words shot out of Scott's mouth so quickly that I was sure that he never took a breath. He bounced as he talked. It was like he had energy surging all the way from his toes to the top of his head.

Scott was a pretty neat kid. I found out later that he went to the same church that my parents had decided on attending. He also lived only a block from our new house.

"Hi, I'm Iza," a girl with dark, curly hair that tumbled down to her shoulders said. She had a really big smile.

"Iza? That's kind of a strange name," I told her.

"Well, the whole thing is Isabella Maria Dominquez. Iza is a whole lot easier for my friends to remember. And this is Kris," Iza said as she pointed toward the blonde, blue-eyed girl next to her.

Kris made Iza's hair look darker, and Iza made Kris's complexion look lighter. As different as the two of them looked, that was how similar they acted. Both of them were crazy.

Kris extended her hand and I gave her five. I liked those three already. Scott was sliding around on the cafeteria bench filled with questions ready to break out of his mouth. "So where did you move from?"

"My family lived in a suburb of Metro City. I think I'll miss all the activities and the mall down the street," I told them.

"You had a mall down the street from your house?" Iza exclaimed. "Why in the world would your parents want to move here from a house so close to a mall? From here you have to drive over a half hour to reach one. And there aren't many stores in this town. You don't get much smaller than we are here. My uncle always jokes that if you blink while driving down Main Street, you'll miss the town," Kris added.

Scott had another question. "What kind of things do you like to do?"

"Basketball is my favorite," I said with a beaming face.

"Great. Maybe you can help us win the championship this year," Scott said. "Do you have any questions for us?"

"Not really. Dr. Wiser was rather thorough. I think that I know the whole school setup now. He told me everything but one small item." I quizzically bent my eyebrows as I said it.

"Fire away. What do you need to know?" Kris inquired.

"Dr. Wiser told me that I got the last available locker, but it is right next to the stinkiest locker I have ever sniffed. It had green goo dripping out of the vents too," I told them.

You would have thought that I told them something

horrible. They sat there frozen. Not one of the three moved so much as an eyelash. "Is everything all right?" I asked.

Scott was speechless for another few seconds, which surprised me. Then he blurted out, "Your locker is next to Hezekiah Bones's locker."

"Who is he? And why doesn't he clean it out?" I asked the others indignantly.

"Hezekiah Bones disappeared more than fifty years ago, and his locker has been sealed ever since. What you really need to know is that there is a horrible curse on that locker. If you so much as touch it . . ." Scott was explaining just as the bell ending lunch sounded.

My mouth was wide open. "What? What happens if you touch it?"

"You become cursed," he whispered the moment before he ran from the cafeteria.

"I've got to get to my next class, but you're in my study hall so I'll finish telling you in there. But don't touch the locker under any circumstances. Promise me that you won't touch it," he warned with a very serious voice.

"Okay, I promise. I won't touch it. But why?" I questioned, but my query didn't reach his ears.

Scott was already racing away from me and down the hall. I put the tray on the conveyor belt and walked slowly with a stunned face to my next class. It was English and following that was study hall.

I was barely able to keep my mind on what the teacher was saying. Of course, she kept looking at me to make sure that I understood all that she was explaining. I think my smiles convinced her that I wasn't in some dreamland.

The truth was that all I could think of was Hezekiah Bones, the smelly locker, and the curse. How could people get cursed by just touching the locker? But if it was true, how was I going to last the rest of the year without touching the locker next to mine?

When the bell rang, I was through the doorway before the other kids could even rise from their chairs. I checked in with the teacher monitoring study hall. It really wasn't a great room to study in. It was the school's auditorium.

My eyes roamed over the rows of seats for Scott's face. I didn't see him. All I saw were torn, old brown theater seats wherever I looked.

At that point, I wasn't worried about trying to find a comfortable seat. I had a curse on my mind.

Suddenly, out of the corner of my eye, Scott entered the auditorium. I moved his way as he slid into an aisle seat.

I dropped into the seat next to him. "You've got to tell me about the curse," I demanded.

"Be quiet or the teacher will move you away from me. I'll tell you later," he whispered.

I sat tapping my foot until the teacher left. The moment his back was out of sight, I leaned near Scott and demanded, "Now! Tell me now!"

"Okay, I'll tell you, but I want you to know that there is a curse on anyone who even tells the story. I'm probably going to get zapped somehow," he said with serious-looking eyebrows that bent low in the middle of his forehead.

"What kind of curse will you get?" I asked out of polite consideration for him.

"It isn't too bad. I become invisible for a day. No one can hear me or see me. Just think of all the trouble I can get into if I'm invisible," he told me as a mischievous grin grew across his face.

"Well, if you're not afraid of the curse, go ahead and tell me about Hezekiah Bones," I said.

"Of course. I'm not afraid of the curse. Are you afraid of it?" he asked.

I swallowed hard. I didn't feel very good about the idea of a curse, that's for sure. I blurted out, "Me? Afraid of a curse? Ha! There's no such thing as a curse."

"That's what I used to think too. The locker that stands next to yours has looked and smelled like that for years and years, even before my parents went to school here."

I interrupted, "Why hasn't someone opened the locker?"

"No one can. People have tried, but the moment someone touches the locker to open it, the curse strikes. Besides, no one knows what is in there. Some people say it's the skeleton of Hezekiah Bones, and other kids say it's his victims. I think his old, sweaty gym clothes are in there. Kris has a different idea. She says that the leftovers from our cafeteria lunches are probably dumped in there. She can't think of anything else that could smell so bad," Scott said.

"No one knows what's inside the locker?" I asked.

"Nope. Nobody has been in it at all since the day

that Hezekiah Bones disappeared from the gym floor during a basketball game," he answered.

My mouth was wide open as he continued, "Hezekiah Bones was the greatest middle school basketball player of all time. He was over six feet tall in the seventh grade, but like his last name, he was all bones.

"During the championship game, the Crider Cats were up by only one basket. There were only two minutes left in the game. Hezekiah went up for a rebound and landed hard on the gym floor. When he landed, he broke a shoestring.

"The coach asked for a time-out and sent Hezekiah Bones to the locker room to get a new shoestring. That was the last time anyone ever saw him alive.

"I don't know what happened to him. No one knows what happened. But we know that the spirit of Hezekiah Bones roams our school searching for victims who touch his locker.

"If you touch it, you break out in a red itchy rash, weird things start happening to you, and he comes back and drags you into his locker to rot with everything else."

"This sounds really crazy," I scoffed.

"Yeah, I suppose so, but there is more to the story," Scott told me as he launched into the next part of the tale. "Hezekiah Bones has not been seen in the school, but there have been times when we all knew he was around."

I asked, "How did you know?"

"Wherever Hezekiah goes, a horrible smell follows him," Scott said as he settled back in his seat.

I sat next to him stunned. My family had moved to a safe little town to get away from the big city influences, and I got plopped right down in the middle of a curse. This was not cool at all.

I tried to look at one of my books, but my mind stayed only on the curse of Hezekiah Bones. I was hearing Scott's words all over again in my head when I started to smell something.

Did Scott have his gym clothes with him?

Was someone in the next row eating Limburger cheese?

I didn't see a thing, but the smell was getting worse.

Suddenly, a guy started to gag. The girl next to him screamed that a poisonous gas was in the room.

Then I realized what it could be.

I looked nervously at Scott and he looked at me. "Hezekiah Bones?"

Scott looked pale. He could barely whisper, "He's coming after me!"

SPINE CHILLERS

Caitlin James scoffs at the idea that trouble befalls anyone who touches the locker of Hezekiah Bones, the legendary basketball player who mysteriously disappeared several years ago.
But she's not so sure when she accidentally trips and falls against the stinky locker.

It's too late to drop out in . . .

The Phantom of Phys Ed

SpineChillers™ #5
by Fred E. Katz